"YOU CAN READ THE NOVEL FOR ITS SYMBOLISM OF A COUNTRY ENDLESSLY AT WAR WITH ITSELF . . . OR YOU CAN READ IT AS A STORY OF LOVE THAT WILL FIND A WAY TO SPROUT EVEN IN THE STONIEST GROUND. EITHER WAY, IT SINGS WITH A TERRIBLE BEAUTY."
—*Hartford Courant*

"O'Brien brings together the earthy and the delicately poetic; she has the soul of Molly Bloom and the skills of Virginia Woolf."
—*Newsweek*

"Among all the major fiction writers in English on both sides of the Atlantic, Miss O'Brien is the leading cardiologist of broken hearts."
—Herbert Mitgang, *New York Times*

"One of Ireland's most distinguished writers . . . takes on squarely for the first time the major issue dividing her native land. . . . *House of Splendid Isolation* is at once a thriller, a moral tale and a deep exploration of human emotion. All this, plus a good story."
—*Seattle Times*

"Edna O'Brien has written a novel in which each character's story is a gorgeous shard. That she's able to piece those shards together into a new whole is a testament to the triumph of her vision, and to the tragedy of her country."
—*Boston Phoenix*

"There's no writer alive who sounds quite like Edna O'Brien. Her prose has a unique mixture of darkness and light."
—Jonathan Yardley, *Washington Post Book World*

"Finely drawn characters . . . a page-turning plot . . . a novel hard to put down . . . with implications that will linger in memory when the sheer pleasure of reading is done."
—*San Diego Union-Tribune*

EDNA O'BRIEN is the author of seventeen books, including *A Fanatic Heart*, *Country Girls Trilogy*, *The High Road*, *Time and Tide*, and *Lantern Slides*. Born and raised in Ireland, she currently lives in London.

"A BRAVE AND IMPORTANT WORK . . . A CONVINCING PSYCHOLOGICAL MYSTERY . . . RENDERED IN BEST-SELLING THRILLER FASHION . . . A RESOUNDING WORK THAT IS VIRTUALLY UNIQUE."

—*Irish Voice*

"Vintage O'Brien . . . A novel about the Troubles, but the Troubles as filtered through Edna O'Brien's passionate imagination."

—*The Times Literary Supplement*

"Powerful . . . History frames this ambitious, intermittently beautiful fourteenth novel by Irish spellbinder O'Brien. . . . The elegiac voice on themes of womanly love, the tale's psychological acuity and the re-creation of a haunted landscape . . . O'Brien still works her Celtic enchantments."

—*Publishers Weekly*

"Haunting . . . pastoral calm and menacing tension . . . a terrorist on the run, an illicit love affair, the police cracking a case, and a country caught in a civil war, all converge together."

—*Entertainment Weekly*

"Provides a sentient immediacy of character and place, the power of which remains long after the novel is finished. . . . Her narrative borders on a Joycean stream of consciousness, moving with fluidity."

—*West Coast Review of Books*

"A story as shrewd in its emotional allegiances as it is passionately told. Full of the bloody poetry and violence of Ireland . . . an oddly, achingly sweet novel . . . with bright, brilliant moments of color from O'Brien's palette."

—*Boston Sunday Globe*

"A kind of *tour de force*, a brilliant experiment in political fiction."

—*Irish Times*

"Surprising . . . a thriller to the end."

—*Vogue*

"POWERFUL AND LYRICAL . . . O'BRIEN IS BOTH AN OBSERVANT CHRONICLER OF SOUL-SQUEEZING IRISH PROVINCIAL LIFE, AND A VIVID PORTRAITIST OF INNER CONSCIOUSNESS." —*Philadelphia Inquirer*

"O'Brien's prose is so rich and original, her characters so urgently present, that a strange kind of elation is induced reading about events that arouse our deepest fears." —*Mirabella*

"O'Brien's first concentrated treatment of the Troubles—and the pain they visit on the Irish people . . . unfolds in a lyric swell."
—*Kirkus Reviews*

"A vivid sense of place . . . interlaces Irish myths, songs, legends, and diary entries with the tale of an escaped terrorist."
—*Miami Herald*

"Should come to be reckoned among O'Brien's best. . . . The reader thrills to the suspense and gets the feeling of having tasted the tragedy that seems to be peculiarly Ireland's."
—*Washington Times*

"Lyrical, passionate, intense." —*Christian Science Monitor*

"A timeless, deeply moving story." —*Anniston Star*

"Brilliant . . . unforgettable . . . great power . . . with the heart and craft of a true artist." —*The Columbia State*

"Shocking, disturbing, yet oddly touching. . . . A subtle, deeply felt, and often beautiful novel." —*Irish America Magazine*

"Impressive . . . offers up sympathetic and illuminating glimpses beneath the surface of Irish life." —*Wall Street Journal*

Also by Edna O'Brien

Time and Tide (1992)
Lantern Slides (1990)
The High Road (1988)
A Fanatic Heart: Selected Stories (1984)
Returning (1982)
A Rose in the Heart (1978)
Mrs. Reinhardt & Other Stories (1978)
I Hardly Knew You (1977)
Mother Ireland (1976)
A Scandalous Woman and Other Stories (1974)
Night (1972)
Zee & Co. (1971)
A Pagan Place (1971)
The Love Object and Other Stories (1968)
Casualties of Peace (1966)
August Is a Wicked Month (1964)
Girls in Their Married Bliss (1963)
The Lonely Girl (1962)
The Country Girls (1960)

HOUSE OF SPLENDID ISOLATION

Edna O'Brien

A PLUME BOOK

PLUME
Published by the Penguin Group
Penguin Books USA Inc., 375 Hudson Street, New York, New York 10014, U.S.A.
Penguin Books Ltd, 27 Wrights Lane, London W8 5TZ, England
Penguin Books Australia Ltd, Ringwood, Victoria, Australia
Penguin Books Canada Ltd, 10 Alcorn Avenue, Toronto, Ontario, Canada M4V 3B2
Penguin Books (N.Z.) Ltd, 182–190 Wairau Road, Auckland 10, New Zealand

Penguin Books Ltd, Registered Offices: Harmondsworth, Middlesex, England

Published by Plume, an imprint of Dutton Signet,
a division of Penguin Books USA Inc.
Published by arrangement with Farrar, Straus & Giroux, Inc.
For information address Farrar, Straus & Giroux,
19 Union Square West, New York, NY 10003.

First Plume Printing, June, 1995
10 9 8 7 6 5 4 3 2 1

For permission to reprint from previously published material, the author gratefully acknowledges Clare Heritage and Martin Nugent for *The Valley of the Black Pig*. Gerald Madden for *Holy Island*, Sinead de Valera for *Irish Fairy Tales*, and the Estate of Shane Leslie.

LIBRARY OF CONGRESS CATALOGING-IN-PUBLICATION DATA:
O'Brien, Edna.
House of splendid isolation / Edna O'Brien.
p. cm.
ISBN 0-452-27452-4
1. Man-woman relationships—Ireland—Fiction. 2. Terrorists—Ireland—Fiction. 3. Widows—Ireland—Fiction. 4. Ireland—Fiction. I. Title.
PR6065.B7H55 1995
823'.914—dc20
DLC
for Library of Congress 94-47256
CIP

Printed in the United States of America

For St. Patrick did only banish the poisonous worms, but suffered the men full of poison to inhabit the land still; but his Majesty's blessed genius will banish all those generations of vipers out of it, and make it, ere it be long, a right fortunate island . . .

—SIR JOHN DAVIES,

Attorney General of Ireland, to the Earl of Salisbury, 1606

We have murder by the throat.

—LLOYD GEORGE,

after dispatching the Black and Tans to Ireland in 1920

The Child

History is everywhere. It seeps into the soil, the subsoil. Like rain, or hail, or snow, or blood. A house remembers. An outhouse remembers. A people ruminate. The tale differs with the teller.

It's like no place else in the world. Wild. Wildness. Things find me. I study them. Chards caked with clay. Dark things. Bright things. Stones. Stones with a density and with a transparency. I hear messages. In the wind and in the passing of the wind. Music, not always rousing, not always sad, sonorous at times. Then it dies down. A silence. I say to it, Have you gone, have you gone. I hear stories. It could be myself telling them to myself or it could be these murmurs that come out of the earth. The earth so old and haunted, so hungry and replete. It talks. Things past and things yet to be. Battles, more battles, bloodshed, soft mornings, the saunter of beasts and their young. What I want is for all the battles to have been fought and done with. That's what I pray for when I pray. At times the grass is like a person breathing, a gentle breath, it hushes things. In the evening the light is a blue black, a holy light, like a mantle over the fields. Blue would seem to be the nature of the place though the grass is green, different greens, wet green, satin green, yellowish green, and so forth. There was a witch in these parts that had a dark-blue bottle which she kept cures in. She was up early, the way I am up. She gathered dew. Those that were against her had accidents or sudden deaths. Their horses slipped or their ponies shied on the hill that ran down from her house. She had five husbands. Outlived them all. I feel her around. Maybe it is that the dead do not die but rather inhabit the place. Young men who gave their lives, waiting to rise up. A girl loves a sweetheart and a sweetheart loves her back, but he loves the land more, he is hostage to it . . .

Gurtaderra is the Valley of the Black Pig. The last battle will be fought there. The Orangemen will meet the Irish Army at Cloonusker and Sruthaunalunacht will run blood. The Irish will be driven back through Gurtaderra and Guravrulla, but the tide will turn at Aughaderreen and the Orangemen will be driven back and defeated. In the morning it would be as easy to pull an oak tree out of the ground as to knock an Orangeman off his horse, but in the evening a woman in labour could knock him with her shawl.

It says that in the books.

The Present

". . . Bastards . . . bastards . . . baaas . . . tards." He says it again and again in each and every intonation available to him, says it without moving a muscle or uttering a syllable, scarcely breathing, curled up inside the hollow of a tree once struck by lightning; cradle and coffin, foetus and corpse. Bastards. English bastards, Free State bastards, all the same. Dipping, dipping. The helicopter wheeling up in a great vengeance, giving him a private message of condolence: "We've got you, mate . . . We've got you now," and the lights madly jesting on the fog-filled field. They'll not find him. Not this time. He has nine lives. A fortune-teller told his mother that. Three left. He scrunches himself more and more into the tree. Lucky not to have sprained an ankle or broken it when he jumped. Jumped from the moving van, said nothing to his comrades. They all knew. The game was up, or at least that bit of the game was up. A car tailing them from the time they left the house. Someone grassed. Who. He'd know one day and then have it out. Friends turning traitor. Why. Why. Money or getting the wind up. Deserved to die they did, to die and be dumped like animals, those that informed, those that betrayed. Bastards.

The grass smells good to him, and after three months cooped

up in a house in a town, he's tuned to the smell of grass and the fresh smell of cow dung, to the soft and several lisps of night. He knows his country well, McGreevy does, but only in dark. The dark is his friend. Daylight his enemy. Who set him up. Whom can he trust, not trust. When the fucking Valentino pilot gets tired of his antics in the sky he'll make his way, in near the ditches, across to the pinkish haze of a town. He'll skirt it and go on South, the sunny South. This journey he will make no matter what. He is the sole player. His to do. Even if it's his last. The whirr comes near and far like sounds heard in a half sleep. The fuckers. Wasting their dip lights and wasting their fuel. His mates in the van are protoplasm now, which is why there was no time for the sweet goodbyes. War in the sky and war on the ground and war in his heart.

He says the rhyme that he knows to calm himself. It is his jingle, it sees him through, except the bastards in the beetle are doing cartwheels in the sky, trying to frighten him, to get him off course.

"Daddy's home . . . Daddy's home."

What sort of mood would Daddy be in? Sometimes they can tell by the slam of the car door. Sometimes not. Rory. He walks into the hall past his wife and towards the lounge, where a tea tray is laid with cups and saucers and scones.

"Did you get the fuel for the barbecue?" Sheila asks.

"I didn't."

"I asked you."

"I didn't," he says, and takes a bite out of one of the scones, then drops it and asks what time is dinner.

"Never anything I want, never ever, except what time is dinner."

"You live in clover," he says, and gestures to a new carpet, the cuckoo clock, the sideboard crammed with ornaments, antiques he has paid for with his blasted sweat and his blasted arse. Women. Goods. Wardrobes. Finery. Jewellery. Lolly. There was a time when this avarice of hers was a charm in itself and never did he go for a trip or do a job without bringing back some little thing to hang on her. Once it was a golden seal that she thought was a duck and they laughed buckets over it, which was how the nickname Duckie had come to her. There were lots of little things like that.

"How do I cook this thing?" Sheila says, returning and holding up in its bloodied bag the shins of the deer he had shot a month before. They were sick of eating it. Rory loved to get up early on Sunday morning and go into the woods with his rifle, to track and shoot deer. She never knew whether it was the pure sport of it or whether it was for another reason, and she never asked. There were things you did not ask a policeman that you were married to. A war of a kind was going on, though no one admitted it, a war in bursts, young men coming down from up North, coming down to rob banks and post offices, postmistresses in lonely stations in dread of their lives, ordinary folk too in dread of these faceless men with their guns and their hoods. One had been shot dead on a road not far away. It was in the papers, a photograph of the very spot, details of the rounds of ammunition, the nickname of the victim, his comrade who got away, who hijacked a timber lorry and held a guy at gunpoint for three hours. It was well known, well reported, discussed again and again: the number of rounds fired, the angle at which the Guard shot, the type of wound, the length it took your man to die. Later the Guard was awarded a medal for valour, one of the very few. They met him at a dinner dance and shook his hand. Men like him and her husband lived with that eventuality and it's what made them edgy, made them worry about a mystery caller or look under their cars when they went out. Once, she had asked

Rory what he would have done if he had been that policeman and he said the same, the very same, it's either them or us, him or me. For the most part, of course, life was uneventful and Rory's weekly adventure was Sunday mornings, getting up at five and going off to shoot deer. It got him out of the dumps. He hated his boss and hated the other Guard. The three wise men, they were called. In a small barracks, bickering. The deer that he had brought home made a little trail of blood up the path, and somehow she could never forget it on account of its delicacy. The children watched while he made a big show of skinning it, then cutting it, then making parcels for the deep freeze. The children wrote the labels but weren't sure which bits were which. She would be glad to see the end of it.

"I said how do you want this cooked," Sheila said, holding up the bag fuzzed with blood, which looked gruesome to her.

"Stew it," he said. He was in a foul mood. Manus had put the boot in with the superintendent and blown his chances.

"There's no need to snap," she said.

"I'm not snapping," he said, and looked at her with a sort of apology. At least she kept thin. Every day he battled with his damn weight, and now it was his teeth killing him.

"The abscess in my back tooth is flaring up again," he said, and tapped his tooth with his ringed finger. It was a Claddagh ring she had given him and he had said when he put it on that he would never take it off, that it would go with him wherever, whatever, and it did, for all eternity.

"What's Manus up to now?" she said, softening a bit. There was no point in these rows; they had a nice bungalow, enough to eat, their children were hardy, and all who visited commented on the beautiful view, were offered a look through the binoculars and told to veer in on the various sights on the lake—stone monasteries and oratories, the several islands, the houseboats moored on the far side, mostly white boats.

"I'm stuck . . . We're stuck . . . Thanks to Manus."

"How do you know?"

"Because I read the minutes."

"What did they say?"

"Oh, Manus talk, how I lacked vision . . . Visions . . . I stop people for nothing . . . I am uncouth . . . I am unpopular."

"We're all right . . . You love going up the country, going into the forest and shooting deer," she said, taking his part now and going with him in imagination in the early morning to the wooded tracks under the purple mountains, a moistness in the air, young trees and old trees dripping, astonishment when two or three of these haughty creatures appeared and stood still, then the bang-bangs, one of them felled, the remainder vanishing like wisps of smoke. He had described it to her once in bed and she had liked it, heard another voice altogether, softer, deeper, and somehow truthful.

"Manus . . . My bête noire."

She knew what he meant. Knew that Manus had it in for him since that time when he arrested the wrong man for the anonymous letters. Was sure it was that man, that Englishman who had come in a caravan to live. Sure it was him with his ponytail and his earring and his homemade beer. That Englishman. Pornographic letters sent to one woman after another, disgusting. He thought he had the man a dead cert, except it turned out he had the wrong man, and for that he was put over the coals.

Without addressing either his mother or father Caimin crossed the room and turned on the television. A cure for dandruff featured a wife rebuffing her husband's advances, but sometime later his dandruff-free hair made him irresistible.

"That bloody thing," Rory said, and shouted to his son to turn it off, when his whole world, the one with Manus, the one in the forest in the morning, the one with his wife when they lay down together, the one alone after she had gone out to work in the morning when he pondered, the one when he went to confession, all the worlds he had known suddenly went on revolve.

"Jay-sus . . . Christ Almighty . . ." He was up and crossing over to make sure that this was not a mistake of some kind; he was listening to the announcer telling in a dry and polished voice how a terrorist had got away, had jumped from a moving vehicle and disappeared despite dog and helicopter search.

"Fucking imbeciles," he said.

"Rory!" his wife said curtly.

Kneeling now, close to the set, he asked the lady announcer who was reporting war in another part of the world to tell him how the British Army, the Royal Ulster Constabulary, the Garda, and an entire operation could let a guy who had got away before, who was known to be a pimpernel, go into a field and vanish. How, unless he was a fucking buccaneer. Even in his outrage he gave the fella credit and said, "That's my boy McGreevy, that's my baby."

"Maybe he's a spaceman," his little daughter Aoife piped up.

"I hope he comes this-a-way," he said, waving his fist at the television.

"I hope he doesn't," Sheila said, reminding him of the foreigner who had given masses of employment and who was taken hostage for almost three months and was now having to have treatment in Cologne or wherever he came from.

"We don't want him this-a-way," she said, and put her arm around her little girl as a protection.

"I thought we agreed never to talk shop," he said.

"This isn't talking shop, this is self-preservation," she said, and stormed out, adding that if he wanted dinner he could cook it.

"Cúchulainn did that, Daddy . . . He ran the length of

Ireland, kicking a ball," Caimin said, remembering a hero from his schoolbook.

"Don't you be getting any ideas," Rory said, and looking around at the room he saw the emblems of his youth, his proud youth, the cups and ribbons, trophies from his great athletic days, and he thought of the young man leaping out of a moving car and the thrill, the thrill that was part and parcel of danger.

"Ducks," he said through the open door, "don't bother with the damned shins," adding that he'd pop down and get a takeaway and they'll have an al fresco by the fire.

"I don't like curry," Caimin said, and asked if he could have crisps.

"I thought we were saving for Christmas," Sheila called in.

"What's that wine you like . . . that Bulgarian?" he said, and before she could answer, he was out the hall door with a stride, a stride in which he tried to imitate a young man who had sprung from a moving car, and he remembered the hero he had once been, the adrenaline when he went out on the pitch, the puck of the hurley, the slithering, the crowds roaring, the goal, the goals, his wizardry and the adulation of the crowds booming in his ears.

The manure bags don't soak up the wet, but at least they are cover. Three plastic bags and a manger of straw. Like Jesus. Not that he's praying. Others pray for him, but he does not pray; he's seen too much and done too much and had too much done to him to kneel down and call on a God. Some of what he's done he's blocked, he's had to, but inside, in the depth of his being, he feels clear and answerable and circumspect.

A few hours' sleep and the damp will have dried into him.

If they took an X-ray of him he would be all water, all rain. His two mates will be being buried now, the flags, the national anthem, the salute, and that's it. Forgotten. He's had deaths in his own house, so he knows what it is through and through, and still they call him an animal. Well, insofar as he sleeps in a manger, he is one. A child's coffin, a wife's coffin, he's seen one but not the other. He's seen the child's, brought, handcuffed, police on every side, searching the white habit for explosives. Couldn't look at the little face, the little bundle of frozen wisdom that played games with him in the jail on visiting day, hid under the chair when it was time to go, went missing, said she was missing Minnie Mouse and her daddy was Mickey Mouse and he needed her to stay all night. With the angels.

He scrapes the muck off with the end of a spade; the water from a pan that he found under a barrel is brackenish and tasting of galvanise, but he drinks it all the same. His hunger has gone. If they come and find him, that's it. They won't break him. They know they won't. They know that. Jumpy lads, all lip, giving statements, one statement and then another and another. Can't take the heat. He can take anything, heat, cold, even the electric wires flaring his inner temples. The certainty runs deep. It has to. It's all he has left.

Half-asleep; the fields he's crossed and the drains he's fallen into come weaving in over him. He thinks he's eating hay, chewing it like a cow, and then chewing the cud. Who shopped him? The ones to trust and the ones not to trust? Like a terror that comes over them, as if their Maker told them to balance the books. Touts. Traitors. Warmer now. Not the warm of a bed or her body but a dank mineral warmth. He'll know one day and he'll settle up. Sleep, Jesus, sleep. Straw streaking across his face and his mind spinning like meat on a spit.

"What the feck . . . What the feck . . . They're here." He

reaches for the rifle next to his chest, his finger at one with the trigger. Through the narrow slit in the stone wall of the loft he sees nothing, neither a vehicle nor a figure. It's a cow—moaning for all she's worth. All he bloody needs. Where is she? Where are you?

"Where are you, Peg . . . Peg?" he says. Why he calls her Peg he does not know. The sound is low, long-drawn-out, enough to alert the farmer, his dogs, duck squads, the lot. Peering over the ladder he sees her down below, too big gormless eyes moiling in her head and her body in spasm. She has come in to calf.

"Fuck's sake," he says as he stands close to her, the breathing now in laboured and hollow groans. The hooves of the calf come prodding out, then recede, then more moans as he grips her and tells her to push, in God's name to push. He tries holding her hindquarters, but she buckles and thinks to make for the out-of-doors, and the movement, so sudden and unwieldy, makes the youngster inside go berserk. He can hear it kicking, desperate to escape, and holding the mother now he talks to her, says things to her, to silence her moans. The racket inside is like luggage being slung about in a suitcase. It's tearing at her. Her contractions thick and rapid and agonising make no difference at all. The calf is too big—nothing for it but rope.

He finds some and coils it around the jutting hooves, then shoves it up inside her so as to grip the shins, all the while saying these idiotic things. From the gate he uses as leverage the moans follow him, something primeval in them, the moans of the cows and cattle of ancient times, for which land and fiefdoms were fought over. She can't do it. He can't do it. The hindquarters and the hips are knifing her. He has to be tougher. He pulls the gate back a few more inches, knowing he will either break the legs or manage to haul it out, and when the clatter hits the cobbles he is unable to suppress his joy. "It's out . . . It's out." A grey, jellyish stripling in her sack of grey. As he begins to wipe the slime off her face she gets up, staggering at first, then feels her legs, flexes herself, hardening to the wonder of life. A brown calf with a white spot on the forehead, the shape of a V.

"You divil," he says. The mother starts to lick, licking with a terrible assiduousness, licking then spitting out the glutinous stuff, with such relish, such happiness, and he thinks, After all that agony, the love, the impossible licking love of it.

They are not army boots but a farmer's, muddy at the tops, an agitated man rushing in.

"It was a tough one," he says. Better to speak first. The man looks at him and he knows by the look that the man has his measure but says nothing.

"She went out of the house . . . We were watching but she got out . . . One of the girls left the shed door open."

"She had a hard time."

"You did it with the rope?"

"The only way to do it," he says, and goes up to the loft to get his rifle, knowing that the man is watching.

"You're off," the man says as he comes down, his holdall bag folded prudently and slung over his shoulder.

"The afterbirth hasn't come yet," he says.

"It takes at least an hour," the man says and then, "Far to go?"

"A fair few steps," he says, and looks at the cow and gives her a wink, as if to say, "That's a greedy child you've got."

"Would you like to come back home and have something to eat?" the man asks in a tentative way.

"Are you sure?"

"Oh . . . It'll be fine," and the words trail away as if he has been throttled.

Except that it is not fine. The woman knows.

"This is Frank . . . and he would like something to eat," the man says to a woman who personifies greyness: grey hair, a wraparound grey apron, and black-grey eyes, like periwinkles.

"He'd like something to eat"—her voice dry and tart as she muses pitilessly on the stranger's plight.

"He delivered the calf for us . . . A fine wee calf . . . Isn't she, Frank?"

"A big calf," Frank, as he now is, says, and thinks it a good and harmless name to take with him on his journey, and in his mind he tries out suitable surnames to go with it. He does not know whether to sit or stand.

"An army lorry went by a while back." That coupled with a look of bristle confirms that there will be no feed, no anything.

Her husband follows her to the scullery, where she recommences scraping the paint off a shelf with a chisel. He can see them through the open door. At first the husband whispers, but soon tires of it and tells her to get the chip pan and some eggs and be smart about it, and without deferring to him she does.

She watches the stranger with a mixture of fear and terror whilst her husband asks if he is fussy about his eggs. She has left it to her husband to do the frying; all she has done is lay the stuff on the side of the stove.

"It's grand as it is," Frank says.

What else could he say, a hungry man, a murderer, a hungry murderer. Violent emotions are battling up in her while her husband hoists the frying pan off the fire, holds it aloft, and fixes her as if he would pour the boiling fat over her feet. With some sort of grizzled smile she tells the stranger that they have children, four in all, two in South Africa and two at home, and how it stands to reason that she is more worried about the ones at home, what with, what with . . . She does not finish the sentence. She does not have to. Her husband ministers by filling and refilling his teacup and remarking on the size and sturdiness of the calf.

"They always manage on their own . . . Cows always manage," she says savagely, asking both men to think for an instant on the killing instinct of man as opposed to the child-bearing instinct of womankind.

"This one would not have managed . . . Except for Frank here . . . He had to get ropes," her husband says, and puts the pan directly onto the tablecloth, so that Frank can dip his last bit of bread.

"Cows always manage," she says, and goes back to the scullery, making much of her task with the chisel.

After he has gone she looks at her husband with that cold, undeviating level stare of hers, but does not say a word.

"If you lift that phone . . ." he says, seeing her dry her hands.

"Try it," she says, her back to him.

"I'll strike you dead," and he gives the dresser a series of wallops with his belt so that pieces of crockery, some big, some not, fall about the floor, followed by showers of hard and clayey dust. He breaks what's there. She stands, her back still to him, and after he has delivered the final blow she turns, kneels, looks at the strewn pieces, and out of them all selects something she loved, a cream jug, with cornflowers on the front, and like a child with a jigsaw, she starts to put the pieces together. The loss of it is the one soft thing he has seen in her in years.

"It's you and your like that keep them going," she says.

"He didn't harm us—did he?"

"No. He didn't fancy meat, it being a Friday," and gradually the shattered pieces begin to take the form and shape that they once had, except that there is a futility to it, like putting the pieces of a dismembered corpse back together.

"I'm not for them, Julia . . . I'm as opposed to them as you are"—he wants to say it, but he can't, the words stick.

"You'll be met at a sawmill beyond Tuam."

"You're going to have to give me some money."

They stand at the far end of the car park, away from the dance hall, where a jerky succession of lights, crimson and puce, bounce off the windows and make his eyeballs fritter, used as he is to dark and half-dark. He'll be blind soon. A girl with a holy sort of voice is rehearsing "The Holy Ground." She says the same four lines again and again, like she's pulling them up out of her gut, giving birth to them.

You will sail the salt seas over
And then return for sure
To see again the ones you love
And the Holy Ground once more.

Not the usual kind of ditty for a dance hall, something fervent, something desperate in it.

"I haven't got it."

"What the fuck . . . You have a fine car . . . You must have money."

"Funds are not my responsibility . . . That's not why I came. To fund you."

"What the fuck, Iain."

"Roger . . ."

"I can't get down there without money . . . I'm not fucking Cúchulainn."

"Then fucking steal it . . . Go right in there and hold up

the Waltzing Jennifer at the till . . . There's only her and the guy and our songstress."

"I can't fucking do that now . . . Not on my own . . . I don't see you as cover."

"Then you better be going on and fucking steal it somewhere else . . . A lonely widow or a lonely widower . . ."

"I can't go on on fucking nothing. I'm hungry . . . I haven't eaten since yesterday."

From his pocket the man takes loose change, says it's all he has and all he is going to have, and to fucking leg it.

"I'm going to fuck away off someday and chuck this," he says, holding the money bitterly in his palm.

"We'd find you."

"Thanks, Iain . . . Roger . . . I always knew you were a friend," and he is over the low wall that leads behind a bungalow and across the immensity of the dark sodden fields, towards the expanse of mountain, whose crests are moulds of black cloud. The song keeps coursing inside his head.

"I'd finished all the lunches and I sat—I always do—in the back of the van to have a cup of coffee, and suddenly there's this tap on the window, on the side window." She's holding her handkerchief, knotting it, because of being afraid of what the Guard will say to her. He's a middle-aged Guard and he looks stern.

"Go on," he says to her, thinking what dopiness kept her from reporting it for twenty-four hours. Everything about her is getting on his nerves: her stupid glasses, the crop of pimples on her forehead, and a hairband more suitable for a kid.

" 'What's your name?' he said, and I said, 'Teresa,' and he said, 'We're going towards Limerick, Teresa,' and I thought he was joking. And I said, 'I'm finished serving lunch,' and then he slipped back the side of his jacket and showed me the gun."

"And then?"

"I didn't scream or anything . . . He was very soft-spoken. All I did was put the cup down and climb over into the driver's seat, and he got in beside me and we started out and he asked me where I lived and if I was married, if I had brothers and sisters, things about people belonging to me."

"You told him?"

"I had to."

"It's Byzantine . . . It beats all."

"He didn't touch me. Said he was hungry, and I told him that there were cold sausage rolls in the tray."

"And a hot sauce to go with it."

"What could I do . . . He wanted a drink . . . Orange or Coke. He said we'd stop in the next big town and I'd go in and get Coke and cigarettes . . . Silk Cut."

"Why didn't you alert the girl in the shop?"

"I wanted to. I'm sure I showed it . . . I'm sure I was snow white . . . But I was afraid . . . I didn't know what would happen . . . A shoot-out, anything."

"You could be arrested for this . . . For complicity."

"That's what my mother said. She said don't tell anyone . . . Don't tell the Guards," and again she starts to cry and begs not to be arrested, because the fast-food van is their livelihood, seven children and her father on the dole.

"You won't be arrested if you tell us everything . . . Everything."

"He was drinking the Coke and all of a sudden we heard a siren and he sat up very concentrated and he said, 'Take the next turn,' so I took the next turn, up a side road, and we heard the siren going past on the lower road, and then he made me take back roads for about twenty miles and made me rehearse what I was to say if we were stopped."

"Say it."

"My name is Teresa . . . This is my boyfriend, Frank . . . He lives with me and my family . . . We're going to Limerick to a birthday . . . It's not Limerick City, it's up the country and they're not on the phone."

"You should be an actress."

"He said I should learn Irish . . . That it is a most beautiful language."

"You're going to night school?"

She looks up, teary, cowed, and asks if she can go to the toilet.

"In a minute, in a minute."

"I'm going to be sick."

"Oh, go to the bloody toilet," he says, and flicks back the pages to see what little he has written.

"You did nothing whatsoever to let him see that you were opposed," he says as she returns, her mouth a cake of lipstick and the headband off.

"I did," she says defiantly. "I asked him why he'd picked me and he said, '(a) I was a woman and (b) the car registration suited his purposes, and I asked him which was more important, the woman bit or the car registration, and he didn't answer. He chain-smoked . . . Lit one off the other . . . Said he hadn't smoked for three days or eaten, but that he rarely got hungry, he only got thirsty and he never drank liquor."

"Why didn't you report it at once?"

"I don't know . . . Frightened, I think . . . He said when he was getting out, 'I know where you live . . . I know your name . . . I know all your family . . .' So all I could do was drive back off up home. Wondering what I'd tell my mother . . . afraid she wouldn't believe me."

"Why wouldn't she believe you?"

"Because I'm always acting the fool . . . I put stones and frog spawn in the kids' beds . . ."

"You could have been useful, Teresa, you could have been the vital cog in the wheel of detection, and what did you do, you played ball with him."

"But I'm here."

"With nothing concrete; ten times nothing is nothing."

"I'm sorry."

"We'll have to keep the van."

"For how long?"

"A few days."

"I want to ask you something."

"Go on."

"Will he come after me?"

"Why do you say that?"

"They do . . . Once they know you, you're marked for life. You're knee-capped or you're torched." And here she begins to cry, big cumbersome tears dropping onto everything, onto the miserable notes he has made, and he thinks, Torched . . . She hasn't a clue what the word is, but she knows what the fear is and she re-encounters it every time she steps out of her house.

"The van is our life . . . I trained over in England . . . In Surrey."

"There's a woman in there will give you a cup of tea." Anything not to have to look at her, and now this orgy of tears.

Almost night. That dimness when the objects in a room grow shapeless and glide into one another soundlessly.

"Let there be light," Nurse Morrissey says proudly, and holds up the bell for her charge to see, a metal bell with holes in it, and through these finicky perforations a thin, tinny sound can be summoned. She has not rung it, not yet.

The nurse has helped her to transform the gaunt, draughty

room into a makeshift kitchen. There are cups and saucers, biscuits, a tea caddy, condensed milk, a kettle, and a little stove.

"You're much better off here than in that home," the nurse says.

"I don't know why I ever went."

"You had pneumonia, that's why."

"They waken you at all hours to wash you or take your temperature."

"You know what they say—a man's home is his castle."

"Don't go yet," Josie says. The nurse answers with a grunt, then recites her several calls—a young woman scalded herself and a child with boiling gruel, worse than boiling water; a widower with two lots of ulcers, his next-door neighbour raw with shingles; people wanting, wanting poultices and dressings and tablets, everyone wanting, every single one. Mad for talk too. The nurse muses why, the older they get, the madder they are for talk: their past, their present, their futures, anything, everything, afraid of death too, as if she was not afraid of it herself.

"We never know," Josie says.

"Now-now," she is told, and reminded that she can ring the bell, ring it like billy-o.

"Who'd hear it?" she asks, yet rings it wanly, and the sounds come out in stammers.

"Keep you company," the nurse says. "The tinkles are kind of nice."

"A tramp could break in," Josie says.

"He wouldn't stay long without grub," the nurse says in a bluff voice, then reaches to the chair for her oilskin and dons it, snapping the zipper up with haste.

"Well, missus," she says, and tries to sound cheery, as if she was arriving rather than leaving. To think that once this woman wouldn't wipe the floor with her or her kind, this woman with her style and her finery, flashing eyes that matched the deep blue glass of her rosary beads which she dangled in chapel, eyes that brought shame on herself, her departed husband, and another, no longer so; eyes now as insipid and watery as boiled tapioca.

"Allow the tears to fall," she says by way of comfort, and then she is gone. Josie thinks she might come back, because of having forgotten something or pretending to have forgotten something, to soften the parting, but she doesn't.

Alone, Josie scans the room, fixing the objects: the electric kettle, its spout, the biscuit packet, the dreamy sprays in the flowered wallpaper laden down with rose and rosebud, the worn curtains and the curtain pole lopsided on one of its brackets. She tells herself that she is safe, upstairs in her house, in her castle. But are we ever safe?

"Lola . . . Lola," she says. Her butterfly has returned and is fixed in a niche of the wall, folded, like a soft brown pleat; Lola, her only companion, her friend. She thinks of her as female because when Lola spreads her wings her little pubc of dark brown hair glistens and contracts and reglistens. She had thought Lola was gone, escaped between the space and the sash of the window, but now all of a sudden she emerges from under the pink lampshade, circles the lamp, and then whishes onto Josie's face, skimming it in quick patters. It means something. A death, perhaps. She has never given much thought to old people or sick people, but now she does. Her mother's death she effaced from her mind. Her mother dying in the hall of the hospital in a feud about land, a field of theirs that a neighbour claimed as his and which neither family could use because of this ongoing vendetta. It got that tinkers used it, made it their own; caravans parked there night after night, lit fires and drunk people quarrelling or calling their dogs or begging for milk. Yes, in the hospital her mother told her father he was not a man but a weakling, and her last utterance was the field, their field, their rights.

Next time she would ask the nurse for a tonic so as to get her strength back. No one could say what was wrong with her except that she was wasting. How would she have lived her life all over again? People often ask themselves that. Would she have married James, or having married him, would she have made the best of it and borne him a child, a daughter who would be calling on her now, fussing, tending, fetching a shawl or a bedjacket, saying, "Mama . . . Mama"?

The Past

Long ago she had come as a bride, a bride with a loose fox collar over her velvet outfit. She had sat in the pony and trap while her husband, jaunty in yellow waistcoat and pigskin gloves, let the reins go slack, allowing Frisco, the impetuous pony, to canter over the potholed driveway and land them in the back yard, whereupon her husband shouted, took the reins, and steered them around to the second lot of gates, the imposing silver gates which led to the front of the house and which were ceremoniously opened. She took it in almost at a glance: the breast of the house a washed blue and the side gables pointed in bluish stone, stables all along the back, every variety of window in the house proper, some of them bowed, and in the stooping verandah panes of multicoloured glass shot with the sun's rays. The house of the low-lying lake. Any girl would have given her eyeteeth to marry into it.

"The Miss O'Grady," her husband said as she stepped forward, to be introduced to a serving girl who was unable to contain her sputters of laughter. A fox fur on a warm day! Brid was the girl's name. She had a round face and dancing amberish eyes.

Doors and windows wide open, old box irons on the doors

to keep them from slamming, and James's pride in showing her things, marching her around main rooms and lesser rooms and anterooms, saying they could do with a woman's touch, a woman's artistry. In the kitchen a smell of baking—cakes and pies and the Brid one whipping egg whites with a fork, on a soup plate.

Later a stroll in the garden amid the drowsy, murmuring foliage, a cedar big as a house, the bark powdery and pinkish like dye, his name, his age, and his brother's name and age hacked into it with a penknife. Across fields then and over stiles and through some makeshift gateways, past other fields, like seas of waving crimson dock, on down to the jetty, the private jetty of which he was so proud.

Out on the lake in his rowboat, a tartan rug which he had brought over her knees, she saw the sunlight come and go in buoyant bursts and listened to her husband's stories of the lake. The water itself gave her the shivers, the way it crinkled. It was not like a lake at all, more like a sea. He worked the oars calmly, proud to be her gillie, mentioned the names of the islands—Priest Island and Sheep Island and the Island of the Mad Monk, regaled her with stories, people who had stills and made their own drink, families who had lived on some of those islands in his youth, who had had to bring all their provisions over by boat and their livestock back when the time came to sell.

The boat smelt of petrol, and water leaked in on her honeymoon shoes, discolouring the suede, blotching it. He seemed at once so merry and so gallant, and she thought, My reserve, or is it my disgust, will pass, and when we go to bed tonight these doubts will have vanished. She made a list of his good points, his jokes, his smile, his eagerness to tell her the moods of the lake, not unlike the moods of a woman. She remembered her long stint in Brooklyn as a maid, the homesickness when she first went there, looking out at a river, the

East River, and knowing full well that she could not stay there, and she could not return home to a mother who had driven her out because of jealousy and who wrote to her weekly reminding her to better herself or else she would be back in a bog cutting turf. She recalled the first morning in Brooklyn, when she had cleaned the ashes, then polished the stove, then their breakfast, knocking on the bedroom door and being asked to wait, to wait a moment.

"Look, look," James would say, pointing to a bird high above them, a skylark or a buzzard, the spread of the wings outdistancing the body. He knew the birds. He had hunted on the islands. He knew the moods of the water and described a winter in his youth when the lake was frozen and he and his pals skated to an all-night dance three miles away on the other shore and skated home in the morning. He loved nature and he loved his own place and she would grow to love it too, like him be able to tell from the sounds drifting across the water the tap-tapping of the boatman, which only carried when rain was due.

Passing the island with the empty schoolhouse he pointed to a swan's nest, one pair of swans, which, as he informed her, mated for life. Her husband. A man she scarcely knew. Asking then if she would like to go home, and she said yes because her feet were wet. Because of the setting sun the water had gone amber, the same colour almost as his moustache, the reeds like the legs of flamingoes down within it, and further over near the shore it was dark where the rim of conifers formed a black line and were reflected in the water like uneven brush-strokes of pitch. The water was so still that it looked like glass, with here and there bubbles on it, as if spat on. She kept seeing herself in it, her face all distorted.

Helping her out of the boat he used the occasion to pinch one cheek of her bottom, to pinch it hard, and she thought, I can't, I cannot go through with it, and asked someone, some female saint—Agnes it was—what she should do, if she should escape there and then, go back, get her trunks, and run.

"You enjoyed that," he said. She said yes, she did, and remarked on the scenery, the changing colours of the water, the quaint names of the islands and the schoolhouse, which looked sad without scholars in it. He had a joke he must tell her. There was an old man who had lived up at the crossroads and who boasted that though he never went to school he had met the scholars and knew three words in Latin and knew who Archimedes was.

In the walk up the sodden path under the overhanging hazels she felt his eyes on her, on her behind, and regretted each step leading her to the blind and stony darkness that was her future. Her haunches were what he liked best, wide and yet with a daintiness to them. A good mare. She had brown hair, lots of it, and her clothes were of brown stuff, different stuffs, gauze and velvet and voile, layer upon layer of them. He had married her in a hurry, although he had known her for the best part of a year and wooed her in her uncle's pub, where she served behind the counter, winked at her, and wondered if her fur piece was copperish like her hair. Her finery was from America and so was the accent that switched on and off like a tap. Darned for damned and icebox. Far from iceboxes she was reared. Went up to the uncle on the spur of the moment, asked for her hand, and proposed to her and got married in Limerick City without telling a soul, not even the brother. The brother who lived with him, the brother with whom he boxed and drank and argued, would not take well to this glamour puss. Had skulked in the hayshed when they arrived. To blazes with the brother. Her walk and the way she picked her steps between the ragwort filled him with speculation. The brother would have to stomach it and do as he always did: light the fires, pump the water, light the tilly lamps in the evening to take the chill out of the rooms and passages, carry the mousetraps out in the morning and lay them again with rinds of cheese, do as he always had done. Of course he would not be pleased to see his little routines taken over by a woman, to see a woman install herself, to watch a woman go up to the bedroom and imagine her taking off her clothes and sitting in the sitz bath and pouring a can of water down her belly and sponging herself in preparation for her wedding night. She said she liked his moustache. He'd graze her with it, the initiating kiss. She was his first woman, and as his wife she would be both his first and his last.

When they got in from the lake he disappeared. She thought that perhaps as a wife she should follow him, but then thought as a wife perhaps she should not follow. She felt awkward, unsure, and found herself in her unsureness in the dining room looking at things, feeling the curtains, which were a bronze colour and in flitters. She drew one of them slowly along the pole and thought, If anyone was looking in! The glasses in the corner cupboard were many-hued. They were green and red, and some had corresponding oblongs of colour within their stems. The place needed dusting, a woman's touch. She stood on her toes and swung about the room and thought, It is mine, mine.

No mistress, no foreign woman to tell her to do this and do that and don't do this and redo that and why isn't the table laid. Orders. Orders. Her mistress like a sallow sultana in her high bed, her breakfast tray laid before her, the orange cut into eight segments, cut precisely so as to fit nicely into her mouth. From the Ukraine, dark eyes, swimmy, like pools, a command to her bustle, yet knew how to soft-soap her man. Each morning at eight Josie climbed the stairs with their breakfast, or rather climbed twice, leaving the first tray outside the door and giving a little knock to alert them, then going back to get the second tray and entering with her head down so as not to look at them, so as not to hear them with their love and their darling, as they wondered which pastries cook had made. There was a cook, thin and jaundiced-looking, a chain-smoker. She liked the early mornings in Brooklyn, with no one up except maids in houses, maids like herself, cleaning the ashes, emptying the ash pans, doing it quietly on tiptoe, so as not to waken their amorous lordships and ladyships. From one window she could see the water, Manhattan beyond, the tall buildings, pink and ethereal in a haze, like cromlechs of painted Plasticine.

On her day off she walked the streets and looked in shop windows at dress material and lamps and ceiling lights and children's clothes plus children's bootees. In one window there was a skeleton of a little foot, a little dead foot that gleamed like the white keys of the piano. It made her cry. She thought of home then, the bog road, turf being cut, and her family believing that she was living the life of Riley. Riley, when she was in fact a mere skivvy to a plump woman from beyond the Ukraine who could be soft while her husband was around but fuming the moment he left the house in his big black coat and his jet-black hat. Those years were a bad dream now to a woman standing in her room looking out at the wet flower beds, at some bushes turning apricot and briars glutted with blackberries, ripe and unripe. Yes, mistress of a house and a serving girl whom she could call to wait on her, to iron her clothes, to amuse her if necessary. It had rained since they got in. The grass was soaking, and now in the sunshine shadows moved and pranced over it like the hooves of phantom horses. Shadows neither green nor black but sage.

"Oh, those darned shadows," she said as the evening wore on. Things got darker, gloomier, more oppressive. She must do something, do something, run out of there.

She called from her bedroom, where she had been unpacking. "Brid . . . Brid . . . Come up here," she said loudly, anything to quell her foul mood. She asked the girl either to sing or to dance.

"I haven't a note in my head," the girl said, and then leapt into some sort of reel or hornpipe, her stout legs and her black brogue shoes moving from carpet to bare boards and back again, dancing and humming to herself.

What is she thinking? Josie wondered, looking at the pink cheeks and the plaits of hair that bounced like ropes.

"What are you thinking?" she asked aloud, imperious.

"Nothing much." And the girl involuntarily stuck out her tongue. She is thinking of a boy while she dances. The boy's name is Percy. He has told her she has nice eyes. Also that his mother has cancer and will soon die. The nice eyes and the cancer are mixed up. She has met him twice and DV will meet him again soon. Nothing in between. You meet at a dance or a wake and then you don't meet. All stasis until something turns up. First met him at a wake, an all-night event, rich house, no one worrying about the corpse, an auc tioneer; lots of grub, whisky, Percy beside her pressing on her thigh, telling her his mother had cancer, had a camouflage of foam where the breast had been, telling her, and she knowing that he was feeling her breasts and having them and she loved it and wanted his paws rather than his eyes to feel them and pull them like he was weighing meal or sausages in his shop, to squeeze the nipples, coax the juices, then lie with him in some ditch and give to him and take from him as she willed. With each thought she was getting wilder and wetter. In a spin. She danced around the fourposter, crossed the room, went behind the shutter, peeped out, and asked the missus would she care for a dance, and together like dervishes they paced around the room, with Brid thinking that she was dancing with Percy, that Percy was bruising her breasts, except that it was the missus, four breasts being walloped in the bridal suite, the ewer rattling in the basin, and Our Lady of Limerick delineated in gold leaf, looking down at them podgily.

At the end of it and breathless the missus searches in her purse and gives Brid threepence. She will not buy toffees, she will put it to buy talc, to smell nice for Percy, to absorb the sweat.

"Who's the local doctor?" the missus asked then, but vaguely, as if it were an afterthought.

"There's only the one," the girl said. "Stack, Dr. Stack." She thought it peculiar for a woman to be asking about a doctor on her wedding day, put it down to nerves, and thanked her Maker that she was young and that when she slept with Percy it would not be in a brown room with brown furniture and creaks but out-of-doors in the soft unruly underlay of bog and bogland, everything seeping into her, his instrument in tooraloora fettle.

Her husband and his brother, Mick, competed with one another to relate to her the story of the mayfly. They were around the fire, the men drinking. She believed that it was from that night that she incurred a dislike for whisky, a nausea which became confused with her morning sickness later. The dance of the mayfly. Her wedding fable. The white nightdress with its satin streamers was laid out on the counterpane by the heifery girl. No sight of pyjamas or even a pyjama bottom. He would be naked, thin and naked, her garrulous spouse. Whenever he looked in her direction the brother sneered, that, along with the fact that he had not addressed a word to her at supper, made her suspicious.

"Top up, J.J.," he said to her husband, and then poured liberally and sneered. They were drinking from cut glasses; she was drinking sherry, a thinner amber, more citrus colour, but dizzying all the same. The bedroom, the nightgown, the undressing kept assailing her, but still she listened and pretended to be intrigued and said at intervals, "James, you are making it up." It had such undertones to it. "The May Madness," he called it, the dance, courtship, and death of the mayfly. She felt bilious from the dinner, a mutton stew followed by an iced plum cake on which their two first names were written in cochineal.

With the whisky coursing through him and his eyes like revolving marbles, he exults in describing the ascent of the fly from the depth of the lake, this fella coming out of his shell, a young lad an inch long with a tail, and how he and his lady get down to business, his lady bigger, sturdier, the prime mover of the game, away from the water, up into the trees and the bushes, first to dance and soon to mate.

"My . . . my," she said sedately, hoping to restrain him.

"The whole place black with them," he said, his brother agreeing, while also reminding him that the ladies were yellowish rather than black but went black in their debaucheries.

"Correct," he said and, then warming to his story, described the lady, lustier by far, more appetite, hoisting her man up, up above the trees to mate, then dancing and mating and what-elsing for two days, and on the third day, with piles of eggs in her, making the journey back onto the water and dropping down and hitting the water and every time she hit, more eggs, more progeny.

"J'ysus, more eggs," the brother said, touching the bride's beige stocking while pretending not to.

"Till she has herself completely and utterly laid," James said, and looked at his wife, the colour rising in her cheeks, and thought his brother, the strong and silent man, his virgin brother, would be the one to take those stockings off, to peel them down, with the same knack as he had skimming the cream off the pans of milk.

"Do the males die too?" she asked stiffly. His brother and

he conferred without words, then burst into laughter. Do the males die too, the brother repeated. They had never dwelt on that before, but reckoned that the males died too, poor buggers.

"But it's the female that makes the play and does the tricks," James insisted.

"Until she's completely laid," the brother said, and looked at this woman, this sister-in-law, and wondered how she would be in time, less standoffish, humbler perhaps.

"Marvellous," James said, and redescribed them, convening on the trees and dancing and mating, mating and dancing, like showers of locusts.

"Around six or seven is when they go down to the lake," the brother said.

"To their downfall," Jamie said.

"She hits the water and lays," the brother said.

"Up again," Jamie adds.

"Drops again," the brother says, "and lays."

"Up again," Jamie says, and does elaborate movements with his hands to signify the laying, the drop, the re-laying, and finally the ultimate descent.

"They call them nymphs," the brother said.

"What do they eat, these creatures?" she asked, moving her crossed legs to the far side of the settee.

"They don't eat," James said, adding that their lives were so short they did not need to eat.

"The fish eat . . . They suck on the flat-out dead female . . . They love her," the brother said, and this time he looked at her and he did not sneer.

"But they give life," James said, and wondered if perhaps his wife would not have preferred a more romantic story attached to the Shannon lake, the one about the Colleen Bawn, the jilted woman who was drowned and whose death was traced later by the appearance of a corset on the water.

Without warning he rose, pulled her from her seat, their arms a distance from each other, tugging and testing each other's strength as they crossed and trounced the shadows in the gaunt, lamplit room.

"Aren't you the great woman . . . the fine woman. James is a lucky man . . . Of course your aunt and uncle had a hand in it . . . your husband or your husband-to-be up there playing cards and getting the grad from you."

"Have you seen my husband by any chance?" she said.

"What! Seen! And he in the bed with you all night, the lay of the lake house, it will be called."

"He went out early." She only murmured it.

"To cool off. They're like that, him and his brother . . . Wild, wild men, they have to cool off," and he looked at her again and winked and swore, "There'll be a couple of children before long."

"Do you know him well?" she asked.

"What know . . . didn't I drive him around, drive the pony and trap all over the countryside, been in pubs with him, drunk with him, do I know him!"

"That pony is dangerous."

"Oh, frisky Frisco, hence his name," he said, and reminded her that he had been to her father's, that he had waited outside, that he had waited the night of the proposal, and how her husband had come out and was so overjoyed and buoyant that they went straight to a pub four miles away, a pub where they knew they would not only be given drink but given a fry and a bed, anything they wanted.

At each remark he moved his chair nearer to prod her with his finger. She could smell him. The smell made her want to retch.

"Wild cards, him and his brother."

"Yes, they're wild cards . . . and I've no idea where they are," she said, not expecting him to answer.

"Well, they could be in Killaloe now . . . or they could be on their way to Dublin . . . The brother's a great tenor . . . 'The Snowy-breasted Pearl'—that's his theme song," and he touched her again and she let out an involuntary shout and then said sorry. His was the nearest house, which was why she came to it. To her to be abandoned the morning after her marriage was no little thing. She might have to go back to her own people. It was not like Spain, where the custom was to hang the bloodied sheets out, because there was no bloodied sheet, the blood was elsewhere, swirling inside her, purple, incensed.

"So you haven't seen them," she said.

"I thought I heard them flying by," he said, and once again praised Frisco, the daredevil with a bit of Arab in him.

"Mr. Doyle," she said.

"Mister! Good Christ. Paddy . . . that's my name, your humble servant . . . Your husband and I, best friends . . . drinking together . . . canvassing together . . . You've married into the best family in the county." His chair now grazed hers, his thigh inside the greased black trousers pressing on her. She could smell him. He had never washed. A man so close to a lake you would think that he would jump in. On the table were the breakfast things reshuffled for dinner, and the fire was laid. The wood was a bright gold, the colour of a certain kind of mushroom, and near it a can of paraffin oil. He leaned closer and closer, touching her knee to make his point. The point in question at that moment was the mixed ancestry of Frisco, what demon she was out of, what sire. Not everyone could control her, only three people, her husband, her brother-in-law, and yours truly. Each time she got up to go, he pinioned her down. His hands were big hands, workman's hands. He made boats, that had been his trade. His tongue forked like a trowel. He was not a cross man, not a vexed man, but a ravenous man. She thought of Brooklyn and thought what a mistake she had made to come home. The card parties, the card games, the winks from her husband were gall now. Her uncle and aunt, who were promised free grazing, would not find it very satisfying to learn that she was dumped in a day.

"Big house," he was saying, while asking if she did not think it too big altogether, too big and draughty. He traced the various owners for her: the engineer who had built it with workmen in the winter when they weren't farming, built it from a design he saw in a book; a later occupant responsible for the shrubs and flowers, had them sent in a sack from botanical gardens all over the world.

"What?" he said roughly to no question that she had asked, then on with his rigmarole, the house she had married into, up the stairs, into the state rooms, as he called them, rooms where others had slept, husbands and wives, English people and half-English people, and one particular Englishman who had brought an Austrian concubine but got sick of her.

"Is there such a thing as an Austrian concubine?" he said. He was so close now she believed she would suffocate.

"I expect there is," she said, trying not to be too aloof.

"Well, he got sick of this Austrian and fell for an Irishwoman . . . fine tall Irishwoman, and he gave the Austrian the fare home and he brought his Catherine—a whale of a time for the first few weeks, bed and hot toddies . . . matinee and evening—and then she got the lonesomes, his Catherine did, and wanted drives back to the town to her father's pub, and it was all right for a time, and he'd drink and she'd drink with him and they'd be driven home blotto."

He winked and asked how many days she'd been married now, then nudged her and repeated that a couple of children would make James happy, tie him down.

"You think so," she said.

"He loves children," he said, and added that there was no better man and no better gentleman in the whole county. She had come there hoping he might go with her to one of these drinking places and entice her husband to come home, but now she was unable to ask him. Anyhow, he was treating her to sagas of the house, more nudges, his chair scraping over the stone floor and his knee like a clamp on her. First he had to finish about the Englishman who doted on his Catherine, his Catherine, who went back to her father's place on the excuse of having to see a doctor and three days later vanished, had sped to France, an adventuress. He described the Englishman's fury, the bulldozer he bought, and how he proceeded to knock the house down and would have destroyed it but for the fact that a posse of Austrians came to beat him up, so that he had to disappear. Not long after, his solicitor came, and soon the house was sold to another man, a convert who shot himself in the kitchen, yes in the kitchen, the gun on a chair, the trigger attached to his big toe with a string and the barrel in his mouth ready for action.

"Never any children, though," he said, sorrowfully, adding that though her husband's parents had two sons, they died leaving these infant children to be fostered out to cousins, so that the house had not known the cheerfulness of children. So this was the house she had married into, and in that instant she knew what a false picture she had painted of it when she saw her fiancé playing cards and sipping whisky and winking at her. Often he had taken her outside and said coaxing things, said her eyes were blue like the kingfisher's, blue and fast. Fast! She liked that.

"A couple of children, that'll lift the curse," he said. She was striving to get up. He offered tea, whisky, all without moving. She said she was needed, to which he asked, "Where?" In the end, with apologies, she managed to get up, and following her to the door, he touched her upper arm in several places, and then standing in the doorway he lifted his cap and thanked her, thanked her a thousand times for coming and said she was welcome, welcome at any time; then he said her full married name and saw her to the broken gate and said what a good-looking woman she was, kept saying her name as she walked down to the dust road, her heels far too high for comfort. He shouted his thanks again.

"Thanks a thousand" was what he said.

"You have a lovely view here," she said.

"I've no woman, though," he said, and the look he gave her was steeped in both umbrage and lust. She walked smartly, noting that parts of the road were damp and parts not. In the centre the green was very soft, like cress or moss. At moments she looked back, fearing that he would follow. At the crossroads she stood and shook. To be a bride and yet not a bride. To be a wife and so cursorily left; no, that was not what she had wanted, that was not what she had consulted teacups for.

For the last stretch she walked with a great composure to show or to pretend how installed she was in her new realm. A child with dipping bloomers rushed out of a cottage, followed by a drake, doing loud ejaculorums, and in some kind of embarrassment she waved to a woman inside who was washing clothes in a tub.

Going on towards home she noticed that the iron gates were open and thought with relief, He has come back, they have returned.

That was the first time she encountered the gypsy girl. She saw her at a distance, then noticed her ire as she came up the rutted avenue, complaining that a servant had sent her away without either a cup of milk or a ha'penny.

"You must be the new woman of the house," she said, her voice overloud, raspy.

"I am," Josie said, and felt eyes hot and pepper-coloured scanning her up and down. It was what the girl said then that unnerved her, something about the missing pane of glass in the conservatory window.

"Oh yes . . . The wind always dislodges it," she said.

"A man will come in and a child go out," the girl replied in a singsong way.

What did that mean? She wouldn't ask. She did not want to know.

"Not in that order . . . Mark my words." And then her hand, weathered as a piece of pumice, stretched out for the coin, the palliating coin, to thank her for her prophecy.

"You'll have to walk back with me."

The girl walked a few steps behind her, her boot rebelliously kicking the loose stones as she went.

"You shouldn't wear purple, you know." She stood on the front steps, craning so as to see the fixtures and furnitures inside the hall.

"Why not?"

"Some colours bring bad luck."

"You people talk a lot of rubbish," Josie said, retreating, then hurrying back with the penny and a slice of cold pie.

"A man will come in and a child will go out," she said, trotting off and looking down disgruntled at her spoils.

It was a side window of the conservatory which, as her husband said, got smashed, year after year, not by any human hand, but by a hand unseen. He had to admit that it was a bit uncanny, and that the glazier thought the same, said how was it that no type of glass would stay still in that pane.

The smoke-coloured hounds were almost invisible, their shapes melting into the hills and hollows over which they ran. Quick, weird, zigzags, and then a squeal, an identical squeal each time a rabbit was killed. Her husband and brother-in-law decided to put on a show for her, a bit of coursing, when they got back from their spree. They each carried a naggon of whisky, which she was asked to hold when they went to get their prey, the felled hare or the felled rabbit which they carried back as trophies. They laid them at her feet. By the ninth squeal, which meant the ninth killing, she wanted to go in, but Jamie would not hear of it. He decided to adorn her so two were laid on her shoulders like tippets, the fresh blood warm and simmery. They laughed, the men did, wild, sputtery, half-drunk laughs, and her husband said she need never send off to the furriers for a catalogue, they could make her a fur at home, a grey-and-tawny contraption that would knock spots out of any manufacturer's stuff.

"Tell John who you were taken for, on the boat coming home from America," Jamie said, tweaking first her chin, then the warm bloodied snouts of the rabbits. She refused to tell it, and in her refusal they stood testing one another, wondering who in this trio would crumble. Everything seemed to be in waiting: the dead animals, the trees, the fields, and the mountains all suspended in an eerie, breezeless stiffness. Not a puff of wind. Not a drop of rain. No, she would not tell. She arched her shoulder to ease off one of the animals, to show her sovereignty.

"Thought she was Gloria Swanson," James said.

"Ah, stop," his brother said, though he had not a clue who Gloria Swanson was.

"Will you remove these things," she said, flicking her right wrist. That brother would have to go. Two drunkards, too much altogether.

She had nagged him about it. She hadn't married a brother-in-law, a gambler, a ne'er-do-well. Eventually James gave in and called his brother out of the hayshed to tell him there would have to be changes, except that he could not spell out what those changes were. He kept offering cigarette after cigarette and asked whether they should plough the near field or the far field the following day. He could not bring himself to be blunt, to say, "Mick, you have to pack your bags and get out." He hated her for making him do it. He hated the way she lay in bed nightgowned, like a starched mummy. He hated her corsets, pink, laced at the back, metal studs down the front, an armoury.

"Women . . . They're never satisfied . . . You give in to them and your life is hell . . . You don't give in and it's hell anyhow." He said it with his back to his brother.

"I was going anyhow," Mick said.

"It shouldn't happen . . . Shouldn't happen to us . . . Us who were orphans . . . What would our mother say . . . What would our father say . . ."

"I was going anyhow."

"Oh, Mick," he said, but he did not turn round, for the simple reason that he was too ashamed to.

Wet fields, brown clay through the blades of grass, fields like graveyards, undug. She was nine months married and nothing doing. People began to talk. He drank more heavily now, not the garrulous drinking as in the beginning, when he would pour whisky into a cut glass and hold the liquid up to the light to praise it; not even the sullen drinking after the brother left, when he would take one of the good glasses and the bottle out into the fields and drink alone. Now it was different drinking, spiteful; he went on a batter. Might stay a day, a night, a second day or even a third, and eventually they brought him home. He had to be carried in. Sometimes he shouted at her and sometimes he was all jam, complimenting her on this and that, her lace collar, her cooking, her hidden skills, and in it all there was an innuendo for the neighbour or the driver or whoever had fetched him home.

He never tried to mount her on the nights he was drunk, he just slept and roared, and his knees cracked as his shins arched up and down in mimicry of riding his favourite filly, the legs going up and down as if it were the filly's chestnut flanks that he felt and nuzzled. In the morning he mounts her without a word because she has got into the goddamn habit of saying no and stop and no. He has taken to holding her lips shut with one hand, clamping the way he might clamp an animal, and he has grown to like it; he likes the power he has over her, making her sing dumb. He calls her muddy, short for mother and mud, and says lewd things while he rises and rears within her, master of her, man-of-war, as he endeavours to prise her apart, go right into her, up through her, and then into her mouth and out as what, a babby maybe. Only in the last slobbery gasps does he release her lips to hear the no and stop and no.

"You can't stop me now, missus," calling her all the names under the sun, including tinkers' names, and each time thinks, She will have a child, she will have issue, a son. To rile her he asks if she enjoys it, and when she says no or nothing, he takes the shoehorn, the bone one, and presses it into her mouth until she groans and moans and emits a sort of stubborn sound that is neither come nor non-come. She says yes, because she has to, and he chortles because he has possessed her, has had his way. At breakfast he jokes, says to call an arse an arse and not a backside, says what a saucy customer she is.

He does not drink for a week or ten days, until he is ready for her and, in the day or two prior to it, grows tetchy about everything, the milk, the tea, the bread, whether the clock is fast or slow, refusing to go to the shops for commodities, then insisting he will go if he sees her pump her bicycle, and in a sudden diatribe flings the vehicle across the grass.

Up in the village he is a gentleman, talks to people, buys buns for girls, and sings a song if asked. When he isn't buying buns or cracking jokes, there is in his eyes, in all of him, a vacancy, like a lost stunned animal, far from home. He either buys the commodities and returns or buys them and flings them at her, and that night or the next he is gone, and days later he is carried back, and in bed he groans and in the morning he mounts her with a lingual gusto, commandeers her inside and outside, and still and feck it, she does not get with child.

"Thata girl . . . Thata girl." Brid grabs the rump of the red hen, holds her neck to stop her clucking, then with effort eases the egg out. It is a soft egg, same one every second day, because Moira, the hen, has something missing in her, calcium, hence the soft egg, useful, an egg that won't be missed. Brid uses the yolk to put lights in her hair and the white as a face mask. She read that. She flips the white with a fork on a soup plate when there's no one around. Just stiff enough, a bit like something else, like Percy when he starts to bubble in her. Always wants to take it out. She fights him, though. She doesn't want it on grass, wasted; she wants it in her, to give her a glow.

"You'll have a baby," he says.

"I want a baby." She clings to him. Half in and half out of her, he marvels at the hunger, the daring, when she bends and drinks it, every drop of it, saying she'll have it anyhow, she'll have her fill of him. She tells him what it tastes like. Whether it's celery or parsnip or Sunlight soap; it tastes different each time. Percy in a sulk afterwards. He doesn't want a baby. He doesn't want responsibilities. He says she doesn't want a baby either. How does he know? Little mite to hold in her arms, like a doll, only the colour changing in the cheeks, getting red or terra-cotta, little thing crying when it wants food, then not crying, her very own. She'd give it a nice name. Deirdre or something like that. The missus didn't want a baby either. Wore corsets that were too tight. Had to have assistance at pulling the lacings; they had to be pulled until she had an hourglass waist and could barely breathe.

"I've been told by a specialist that I may never have children," the missus said.

All my eye, Brid thinks, and lingers for the sixpence or the castoff that she might be given for doing a favour.

A baby. It cried inside her. She could hear it at all hours. It wasn't thumping, just crying. It was not a normal child. She prayed for it not to be. In the mornings she searched the lavatory bowl for a sign and once roared with delight, but it was a trick of the eye. What she thought was blood was a brown stain on the worn porcelain. It cried inside the walls of her womb. It was more like a banshee than a child. She prayed that she would lose it, that its crying meant it did not want to live. Her husband sent her to the doctor, said she was to get something, he didn't care what, ammunition for her barren loins.

"Your husband is getting ratty," Dr. Stack said.

"I don't see why," she said.

"On at me!" he said.

"Is he on at you?" she said archly, pretending to be surprised.

"That's why you're here . . . Husband's orders and doctor's dilemma," he said, his eyes going up and down the length of her body, assessing her charms. She had a taut quality and she trembled, a woman asking to be broken in.

"You hear everyone's woes," she said.

"Sure do," he said. He liked the way her eyes flashed, like swords. Might he ask what her little woes were?

"I feel quite lonely," she said, and did an imitation yawn.

"How come?"

"Oh . . . Dark evenings . . . Animals . . . lowing in their stalls . . . Routine."

"Ergo . . . You came to see Dr. Con."

"On my first Sunday at Mass here I wondered who the dashing man in the camel coat was." If anyone could help it would be him. He was human, he drank a bit, his patients liked him, and he had a large family.

"Gorgeous," he said, and leaned across to check her for anaemia. When he pulled her lower lids down, she felt something unusual in his fingers, a softness, like the slide of caterpillars off a cabbage.

"You need iron," he said.

He tapped her chest then—quick, smart taps so that she winced.

"I better have a look at the drawbridge," he said.

"Not today . . . Not today," she said, she pleaded.

"Is it flag day?" he asked, and though not sure what he meant she nodded, making a little show of embarrassment by turning away.

"One wants the gentle approach . . . the velvet touch," he said, and ran his hands down her body, searching it inch by inch and pausing to feel the bulk of a sanitary napkin.

"I'll come back another time . . . another time," she said,

begging by her eyes to make him understand, to feel her apprehension, her fears. He saw the tears and asked quietly what was wrong.

"I think I'm just rundown," she said, and referred to the iron tonic.

"I think it might be your libido . . . There's nothing I don't know about a woman's libido," he said, and placed a token kiss with his finger on her brow.

In his motorcar as they stopped to enjoy a view of the lake, the panoramic view, she decided that she would risk it. She would talk code and he would talk code back. Her gloved hand met his on the steering wheel as she said what a comfort it was to find a friend.

"A friend . . . a lover . . . and a doctor," he said proudly.

With a tremor in her voice she said that yes, there was something, but it was not a baby proper, and she begged him to help her.

"Like what?"

"You could give me something, some medicine."

"You mean to flush it out," he said, and looked at her with hate. Was she asking him to collude, seeing as she had opened up to him and got him into a lather, was she asking him to breach the laws of nature, to break the Hippocratic oath, to commit murder?

"I'm not asking you that . . . not that at all," she said, and turned away.

"Are you or aren't you up the pole?" he asked.

"I'm not," she said, and started to weep.

"You should be on the stage," he said, and thrust her off.

His driving now was different, a jerkiness to it, the wet ribbon of road racing towards them, then swallowed up by them; the seat, which needing upholstering, bouncing under her weight. He kept fiddling with the radio knob to get the time and the news. She talked twenty to the dozen. It was about a type of beetroot that her husband was thinking of growing, not an edible beet, one for cattle which according to the booklet preferred a soil with lime in it.

"My husband has a degree in agriculture," she said.

"He'll need it," he said, and came to a screeching halt at the crossroads, half a mile from their house, saying she would have to excuse him, duty called and his dispensary would be full.

"I'll come and see you again," she said, but he made no reply.

"What am I to do," she said, walking down to the gate and then back to the crossroads and then down again, trying to find an answer to her predicament. There was no one she could tell. Her mother least of all. Her mother had always hated her because of the way her father spoilt her, put a cushion on the handlebar of his bicycle and took her for bicycle rides. Her mother used to describe her labour, especially the labour she had had with her, taking a day and a night to get out, bucking around inside her, the head like an iron ball, coming out, going back in again, a stubborn, haemorrhaging head. This child and her mother were one, in league against her. No, she could not have it and she could not not have it. There was no one she could tell. There was no one she could talk to.

Down by the lake her husband could be heard roaring. He brought out the bottle. His finickiness about glassware had gone. Sometimes he took the boat and let the oars drift. His shouting carried to the opposite side. On the shore he paced. God knows how many miles he covered doing the rounds of the fields and the lakeshore and then up to the house and back again, loath to go in. Looking for something. His childhood. The child he did not have. In the mornings, for the rats he had to have a pot of tea in bed and squeezed oranges. The squashed halves of the oranges on the draining board reminded her of her battered breasts. He knew she had done wrong by the way she waited on him, by the suppliance which was new. He knew but he could not tell.

When the delirium tremens got so that every item in his room crawled and black slugs crept out of the wallpaper, she had him dispatched to a monastery forty miles hence. There, over the weeks, he told his story or parts of it in the kitchen garden to a monk who was on a vow of silence and who could only look on, with infinite gravity and infinite bafflement, at a man who said that women were cold, cold, reachless archipelagoes, that a woman could persuade a man that black was white or vice versa. The beads on the monk's rosary warbled as he worked. The days passed slowly, and at night the man moaned and shouted lonesome things.

Paud could not look up at the missus, but rather fixed his attention on her skirt, a grey skirt with a little swirl of pleats around the bottom. He stared at the stitched hearts at the top of each pleat, hearts threaded in grey. He could not believe he was in their kitchen alone with her. Her husband was away on business, she said. She had collared him in the front field, shouted, "You there," and thinking he was about to be questioned about poaching, he ran off. She kept hollering, and knowing that if he didn't stop she would go up and call out his father and create ructions, he gave in.

In the kitchen he was being asked what he could do in the way of farm help. Could he tackle a horse, could he milk cows, could he take the milk to the creamery?

"Maybe," he said, his head down, his orange hair dripping with rain, and his glasses blurred. He could not look at the missus. He wanted to kneel down at her feet and adore, touch the grey cloth with the moving procession of pleats. He had seen her often on her bicycle, and once, on her way to Mass, she had actually fainted outside their cottage and had to be helped up off the road. His mother brought her water, which she didn't drink because the glass was dirty. She didn't say the glass was dirty, but he knew it and saw the disgust on her face as she handed the glass back. Next day she sent up a can of red currants and black currants for them to make a pie, to thank them for their assistance. Could he add? Could he subtract? What did he know of his country's ill-starred history? At once he burst into a recitation of what Miss McCloud, his teacher, had dinned into him and others day after day: how their country, their beloved country, had been sacked, plundered, and raped by the sister country. Miss McCloud spoke of battles and insurrections, big battles and lesser ones, the blacksmith's forge that wrought the pikes and the rifles, then the tragic flight of the Earls, the cream of Ireland's nobility, having to fight with armies in Europe, then Black '47 and Black '48, the creeping death, women gathering weeds to sustain their young, men, decimated men crawling to the stock farms in the hope of being able to procure a portion of bullock's blood for their families. All he could say was that he knew the songs, the rebel songs, and his favourite was "Roddy McCauley Goes to Die on the Bridge of Tuam Today."

"A pig has to be killed this week," she said abruptly.

"My fatha can cut its throat," he said, blinking in the hope that the blink would wipe the water off his glasses. He was afraid he would faint.

"Father not fatha," she said, and made him repeat the word. The stitched hearts at the top of each pleat were ravelling.

"Father," he said unsurely, and prayed to be let out into the damp anonymity of the fields.

He was to start at once; he could clean the outhouses, feed the one remaining horse, and have the cattle in before dark.

He ran halfway up the avenue and then took a shortcut across the field and over the stile to tell his mother his news. Only the night before she had given him a belting, calling him a cowpawn and other names because she had left him with the two children and come home to find the fire quenched, children squealing, and a cake of bread only half baked.

"They gave me a job at the big house," he said, and lied about money. The missus hadn't even mentioned money. His mother said it wouldn't last. She knew that woman well, knew about her moods from Brid. That woman couldn't keep a girl or a boy in her employment, her bitterness and her moods got the better of her. She cited Brid, who was locked in a bedroom for two days and given only dry bread and water, locked in for a theft that she had not done. It was the missus herself who had stolen the scarf, an assistant had seen her doing it, but justice was one thing for the people in the big house and another for the cottiers and the cottiers' friends. She cited the glass of water, his mother did, a gesture that the woman had refused, then a few berries that were hardly enough to make one pie. She cited a man down by the lake, roaring to himself, a man who told passing strangers execrable secrets about his wife.

Paud wasn't listening to this; he was remembering that at one moment in the kitchen, seeing the missus's loose shoelace, he had had this irrepressible longing to kneel down and tie it. They were tanned shoes with little holes in the toes and the lace was darker than the tan. He was remembering this and the missus also asking him if they had rickets in the family, to which he said no, they'd never had rickets, but his sister had scarlet fever once long ago.

"I'll give you a week at the most," his mother was saying.

"Yesterday you said I'd go to a reformatory for boys," he said.

"And that's where you'll end up," she said, and took a swipe at his face, knocking off his glasses.

He didn't care. He'd be beside the missus, in her orbit, bringing her fresh eggs and vegetables. He'd do anything she wanted. He loved her then. He'd engrave her name on the tree next to her husband's. He knew their place well, knew every tree and every clump, knew every little hillock and the fields down to the lake and the boat with the oars that went flip-flop. Green fields and green provinces, except that one province was hanging off. When he was very small he thought he'd be a priest, but later had taken the oath to save his country. That was what Miss McCloud had done for him, and proud of it he was when she asked him to stand up and tell the classroom where the future lies.

"The future lies in a united Ireland" is what he said, is what he believed. Now he had two loves, Ireland and the missus. He'd be bringing turf and logs into the sitting room; he'd see a biscuit box, and if she offered him one, he'd take the pink wafer filled with a putty-like stuff. He'd seen it on the lid in the shop, a picture of each and every biscuit, but he never ate one. He'd seen the ornamental arbutus table; made from the strawberry tree. When the missus was bucking, streamers of pink went up and down her neck. God forbid that he would ever make her cross, that he would ever let her down. He had two loves, two women to die for, Ireland and the missus.

The cause of their ruin. Myopic, green fur on his teeth, couldn't write his name yet brought nothing, only disaster, into their lives. First the fiasco about her corset and then the Republican Bull and her husband going up into a field at night, to bring him away. All very well if the boy lost his life, but no, her husband it was who had to be sacrificed. "Accidental death," as it was called—a cache of arms, a simpleton,

Guards, darkness, bungle, and no one knowing exactly what happened, opinions varying at the inquest, one saying that the first shot had been a freak and she with the black diamond on her coat sleeve having to sit there and listen to Paud say, "I dun nothin . . . There was a few aul guns I was minding . . . I dun know how they got there."

History holding them ransom, when it should all be put to rest in the annals. How often that image of her husband returned to haunt her, his standing in the doorway slightly drunk, his hiccups, his saying that they had a little matter to discuss, that they had to hide Paud, give him shelter for a week, then pack him off to England, to a cousin in Dagenham.

"What has he done this time?" she had asked. He hedged, said he wasn't sure, something to do with leaflets; then it came out: Paud was minding guns in a field for some bloke whom the Guards suspected.

"An arms dump," she said.

"A few blasted guns," he said, whereupon she said not to her house, not to her house, and added that Paud had not enough noddle to mind sheep.

"A week at the most," he had said.

"Those that put him in that field can hide him," she had said, and repeated that her house was her house. How they fought over it, he resurrecting every bit of Fenian feeling that he ever had and she saying that it was out of the question, and his slapping her and hating her not only for Paud's sake but because of the way she had won out with everything, no thoroughbreds anymore, no ponies, the dull slog of muck and mulch and the deeds of the house in her name, the humiliation of being given a few shillings each Saturday like a serving boy. His old rage reared up in him as he took swipes at her, his hiccups going like mad. He had promised he would hide Paud and he was going to do it and that was that.

Fear made her act. Politics were one thing when brave

men were shot long ago for their beliefs, or brave women hid volunteers in settle beds or churns, but politics had become a racket, hijacking, robberies, mindless assassinations. She slipped the anonymous letter under the sergeant's door early the next morning before anyone was up. How was she to know where it would end? How was she to know that her husband would go up that night under cover of darkness, or that the Guards would be waiting, or that her husband would be drunk, or that in the brawl, fire would be exchanged and her husband fatally wounded? Yes, the dark threads of history looping back and forth and catching her and people like her in their grip, like snares.

Going queer then, mixing up flowers and birds, still things and moving things, sucking the spittle from the stems of the wild irises and talking to herself, afraid her husband's ghost was appearing, coming back to accuse her. Did he know it was her? No one knew. Still, she could not go to his bedroom. She slept in the kitchen by the stove and was out at dawn, talking, rambling. Having to be put away for a while. A small room in a nursing home named after St. Jude Help of the Hopeless. Nuns and priests telling her to blot it out, that it was God's will. The odd visitor. Nuns telling her in front of a visitor that she should mix more, that she was too wrapped up in herself. Eventually having to come home and face it, and run the farm and be dependent on workmen and middlemen advising her on what to buy or sell. The vacant, shriven years of it.

Captivity

Night again. The days since Nurse Morrissey left an eternity. No letters in the box by the lych gate, where the postman is supposed to leave them. Too busy to come in. Everyone too busy, not like the old days, when people chatted and lingered. More and more she remembers the old days, all-night card games at Christmas, the dappers who lodged in the month of May, who set off in the mornings for the lake with their picnic baskets and their fishing gear, back at night for their baths and their big dinners; Jamie and herself dancing attendance on them and united for once. One of the wives, a Hilda, a bit spiteful; the men all over her, praising the dinner, the trout they'd caught in blackened butter, roast poultry, and Queen of Puddings, then settling back for a singsong. English people. English songs. "Greensleeves" and "Burlington Bertie, I Rise at Ten-thirty." Jamie singing "Kevin Barry" and no one objecting at all. The old days interred in the mesh of table.

Through the half-opened lavatory window she sees the moon, a curve of frosted lawn, and the gravel unnaturally stark. It looks beautiful, untrammelled, the frost a sheer gauze over everything, and on the silvered grass the fallen leaves and rotten apples stick up like motifs of some kind. She thinks how calm, how constant nature can be. But the stables look deserted in the moon. Seeing them with their doors off, she remembers how she went there to mourn, after her husband died, sat on a stall or a block of wood and drank her cups of tea there. It was as if she could not enter the house, did not deserve the house, even though he had signed it over to her years before. Only in the garden did she feel at home, at home with the weeds and the flowers, blue and yellow flowers making their way through the wilderness of bushes, the lawn a quagmire from animals that broke in through the stile. Once or twice she thought, I'll make an apple pie, and then wondered who would eat it. Poor Jamie. She tried to think of the nice bits, the softer bits, the time when he broke down. Horses were at the root of it, horses like concubines, the napes of their necks lolling over the half doors, their eyes bulbous as eye baths, with a blue film over them, sops of hay falling out of their mouths, the long peninsulas of their faces lonesome until he went to them, went to them, calling them names, pet names. Maybe there was a jealousy in her, but there was also a fear, a fear of the consequences, and much as she hated these thoroughbreds, he loved them. What she saw were wild, bolting animals with foaming gums trying to break down their stalls or break out of them. Every time she saw him go out with the rope she knew it would be hours in the field, man and beast spinning round and round in a kind of ecstatic frenzy, enemies and also friends. She never knew how many he had. Some fillies in fields she never went to. Only from others or from hearing him on the telephone would she learn that another filly was to be dispatched, big talk about dam and granddam and how she was rated by this trainer or that. It had to be. These thoroughbreds having to be fed with the finest grain, given tonics, sent away to stud to be covered; these would be his and her undoing. She saw it coming and yet it was different when it came. Broke down, like a child, the morning he read his name in the *Gazette*, his name and the extent of his debts.

"I'm ruined . . . I've ruined you," he said, and because he cried she was not able to turn on him.

"We're in it together," she said, and he put his hand out and opened his heart to her and asked her to forgive him, to forgive, forgive. His mother should not have died on him. His father ditto. He never stood a chance. His mother and father in their bedchamber day in and day out, lovebirds, had a nurse for the children and stayed in that big room drinking and saying soft things to each other, the very same as newlyweds. He saw his father comb his mother's hair, then brush it, use brush and comb alternately on the long, thick, brown hair while she looked in a hand mirror so that she could see him looking at her, loving her and returning the love in the glass. He hated it. He said that he said "Mammy," and they laughed at such a little boyish plea. His mother took ill. Egg flips brought up to her; he and his brother admitted to the bridal chamber only the odd time, mostly evenings when they couldn't see her. Her voice was weak. Her husband held her as if she was gossamer. The night she died he and his brother knew it without ever being told. People came in ponies and traps or on horseback, and in the passages there was running and calling, the flying flickers of lamps, commotion. Then there was a motorcar. That would have been the doctor. The two children were given caraway cake in their room. He sat on the floor and took every single seed of caraway out of the cake, in anger. My mother is dead, my mother is not dead. He was only three. He said he felt a silence then in direct contrast to the hullabaloo of earlier, a vast silence, some sort of reticence in plaster and beam, then the almighty howling, a husband howling for the sweetheart who had faded, who had died on him; a husband kissing her, kissing the extremeunctioned body and the long pleat of hair, kissing her in order to be one with her, and the children, himself and Mick, witnessing this fevered goodbye and not knowing what it was to hate, but hating this man who had no thought for his children and hating the woman for having had the cruelty to die. Not long after, as if in the gluttony of kissing, his father had sucked death from her, he followed her to the grave, was united with his "Jenny with the light brown hair," leaving orphans who had been allowed to look in on the sickroom, look in on the dead, but never brought in or made part of it. A fecklessness had taken root in him then. She asked, "Is that why you married me, James?" She asked twice. He cried and said, "It could be . . . It could be that," and looked at her with the most pitiful eyes, eyes in which the tears, milk-coloured, were like blisters. They had taken a step and they had taken it together. Seeing him after that sit with the rug over his shoulders reminded her of one of his ailing horses in whom spirit had been quenched. His commandeering of her, the wallops, the Vaseline he smeared on her were all things of the past. They sat side by side of an evening, in the conservatory, numb with cold, until the stars came out and he told her stories, the same stories that he loved to tell again and again, stories about himself, his wild-oats days, telling her not as his wife but as his nice old nurse who used to put eucalyptus on his chest and give him cough syrup off a spoon.

"God rest them both," she says, and wonders why she says it.

She shuts the window, then on impulse opens it again to let in the crisp frosted air, to let it circulate through the decrepit house.

She hears something, not a voice, a thud like a door or a car door being opened and then shut, and yet not that, not that at all, a presence.

"Who's there?" she says. She listens carefully, her heart hammering. She is three, no, three and a half floors up and anyone could break in, though the doors are locked and bolted. There is a note taped to the hall door which says "Please knock loudly and wait. Wait a good long time." She could make her way down there, slowly, with her walking stick, and intends to, except that she believes the creeping is now inside, footsteps, someone already in. She starts to reassure herself, to say that it is most likely birds, crows in the chimneys, or wind. She listens for the wind and hears it come and go in fits, like a mummer, a cold wind blowing in from the lake, over the fields, and stalking the house, obliging her to mutter a childhood ditty: "Oh, wind and rain, bring my daddy home again." She would give her eyes out to have someone befriend her, not her mother, not her sister, a friend from her Brooklyn days, a best friend, or poor Paud, who mended punctures, polished her shoes, and called her to her face "the missus." She tells herself the noise was nothing, a mere hallucination, and how she is in her own house, barricaded in, and how presently she will reach out and push the button of the electric kettle and make herself tea and dip biscuits in it and plan how when this night is over she will bestir herself, she will set about finding a youngster to live in.

All is quiet, a compounded, gathered quality to it as though in preparation. What it took was the turning of the wooden knob, two, three swivels, then a wrench because of its loose threading, the door itself swinging back and forth quietly but with a livid glee, then a face hooded, eyeballs prominent, eyes like grit, and a voice reasoned telling her not to move and not to scream, saying it several times. He lowers his gun when he sees that the only thing confronting him is an elderly woman in a fourposter bed, clutching the strings of her bedjacket.

"Who are you . . . What's your name?"

"Who are you?" she hears herself asking, amazed that speech has not betrayed her, because in all her nightmares it does. Except that this is no nightmare, or rather the substantiated one, the criminal she has read of and has thought of as being chiefly confined to cities confronting her in her bed, his face hooded, his boots and trousers caked with the muck of the country. The debris of three provinces is on them and his breathing is short. There is something animal within the stillness of him, as if he is covered in a tawny fur that cannot be seen or smelt with lay senses. In a voice completely assured he tells his organisation, his rank, and says she need not come to harm if she does as he says.

"Who are you? Who else lives here? Have you daily callers? Do you draw a pension? Have you animals—pets? Does the postman come indoors? When was the last census? When were you last seen up in the village?" Chapter and verse, the questions as automatic as if they were the bullets from his gun.

"There's myself and my Maker," she says quietly. So this is how it happens, this is how a life is suborned, one's insides turned to whey, an opening door, a man, hooded, with not a lax muscle in his being, a loaded rifle, and outside, crows cawing with the same eventide fussiness and no one any the wiser that her time is up.

"Everything is to be as normal," he says.

"Normal," she says, as if to an advocate in the room, the vanished Lola perhaps.

"What have you come for?"

"To lie low."

"Might I ask why, and why here?"

"Never discuss my life or my actions, for your own sake . . . And for mine," he says, and goes out with the same stealth as he came in, no doubt to continue his search and decide where he can best billet himself. For a moment or perhaps longer, a lucidity possesses her, a great white shaft of thought such as when all is annihilation, and then easing herself onto her funny bone, she gets out of bed determined to dress herself.

His limbs scratched and exhausted, he lies on a pallet bed in a downstairs room in the dark and thinks he will take the thorns and briars out of his feet later. He longs for a smoke.

"So this is the woman you raved about, Queen of the Munster Fairies," he says, and laughs, quietly and bitterly, and enacts having a smoke. He is talking to Paud, remembers Paud blathering about the house and the woman, like a lady on a coin with a leash of hounds, her husband and herself martyrs for Ireland. Paud, a bit of a loner, working up North with handicapped children, but eager, ever eager, to pass messages or hand out leaflets or the newspaper at the corner and lamenting the fact that he was too old to join up and do missions. As if he could be entrusted with something as dangerous as that.

"At least you got the house right and you got the lake," he says, and thinks how nice it looked, the moon on the water, the timber jetty, the idly rocking boat. In seven days it will be done, but as with every job he can't think it done until it is done. In the last town a sudden spurt of wind as he came around the corner, relieving him of his stalker's hat and his wig, their veering in two directions, his going for the wig, which had caught on a bit of sewerage, then sallied into a back yard, where he couldn't follow because of a light being turned on. Bad mistake. Bad start.

Nothing for it but to lie low, get some sleep, and not hassle with the woman. Sleep. Sleep. Wasn't there some story about her, some disgrace, her and a priest? Oh, the sunny South, where people had time for love and strawberries, forgot their brothers and sisters across the border, let them rot. Paud full of temper, dying to join up and learn about guns and be given a job and a rank. How little he knew. How little anyone knew when they joined up. How little that woman up in the bed knew with her wild, staring, Virgin Mary eyes.

He thinks of Shiona. So soft a sound. Like silk or a breeze. He grants himself one, two, three fleeting reflections of her, and then he holds his head in both hands and pummels it and bangs it on the iron rungs to blank out the longing.

Maybe he will dream of her, the same dream, her coming through that closed door, that closed and blood-soaked door, calling him. He has never put it into words, through all the long generations of nights and walking and scrapes, because there are no words for it. She is simply there, unscathed and gold like a buttercup. There.

She sits on the rocking chair fingering the white fringe of the counterpane, squeezing, then arranging them in a series like fingers, thinking rash and contradictory things. He will kill her, put her body in a sack and dump it in the lake; he will not kill, one of his comrades will come and do it. He will maim her. He will demand ransom money, except that she is poor and her relatives poor also. Guards will come and raid the house, will get wind of it, and he will be shot trying to escape. He will hook off in a day or two, leaving no traces behind, a taut apparition. It is difficult to believe that she is in her own room or what was her own room an hour before. She looks for Lola, but Lola has gone too, wise to the catastrophe. She keeps reliving it, knows that she knew in every fibre of her being when she heard the first sound when he must have been out there prowling. Why had she not done something then? Why had she not rushed to the phone then? She might now be being brought out in an ambulance and he handcuffed with a pair of Guards on either side of him.

When she closes her eyes he is behind them; likewise, when she puts her fingers to her ears, his voice is there, a chisel, gouging her eardrums. She begs the wind to stop, to cease for a moment in order to allow her to think. Her feet are freezing, yet the rest of her scalds and itches, itches in different places. She is completely porous, everything is going in, in: his voice, the black monstrosity that covered his features, his nicotined finger so at home with the trigger. A sudden thud outside makes her draw her legs up under her, reverting to a foetus.

Maybe comrades were coming to join him or coming to bury some arms in one of the sheds. She had read in the paper, again and again, of people having arms on their land and not knowing it, arms in plastic bags with lamps to keep them dry. She'd go to the phone presently, phone her nephew and simply say come, come. She had done that once when she had pneumonia. He was twenty miles away, but he came when asked. He knew that the place would be his, that there was no one else to leave it to. Folded into a Kleenex are the four sleeping tablets the nurse has given her. They are minute and ridged, not nearly enough to take a life away. What will he do with her? Horrors such as she has read of done to others whose lives were unremarkable until such a figure came through a door and butchery ran amok.

She wore a grimace as if expecting to meet him. She had dressed fully and put on her coat, her brown coat with the heavy astrakhan collar. She was on her way to the telephone on the landing. Its lifelessness conveyed itself to her long before she reached it. A viper, grey-black, a mute in her shaking hand when she brought it to her mouth to speak. She said

"Operator" and spoke the name of the local postmistress four or five times. Then she replaced it. Looking towards the lower hall she saw only emptiness and darkness where the stairs ended, and wondered what room he was in and what he was plotting now. In the lavatory she had another thought, which was that she might poison herself. A bottle of milky disinfectant stood beside the drainpipe and she remembered reading about an actress in California who had taken some such potion and had died, but the death was long-drawn-out and horrific. Wiping the misted window with her hand, she looked out at the night, the empty fateful night, and thought the lawn, the fallen leaves, and the gutted apples no longer resembled those she had seen a few nights before, everything blemished at his coming.

Later on she thought strategies. She said brave and audacious things. She said that if her husband, James, were alive this would not have happened.

"If my husband, James, were alive this would not be happening," she said, and commenced a letter. Then she sat and used up page after page of the best stationery that had been a Christmas gift and that she had vowed to be sparing with. The first draft said, "I am appalled to find that you have invaded my house," but recalling the hooded face and the pitilessness that dwelt both in the eyes and in the black blank monstrosity of the hood, she decided to write something a little more conciliatory. She said that it was a shock to find someone in her home. Home sounded prim and gentrified, a word calculated to enrage him. What did he and his organisation want—was it the land, the yoke of history, or was it rage in the blood?

No sound, only his breathing and hers, a distance away, three-and-a-half floors to be exact. What was he intending to do? How long was he intending to stay? Did he mean to use the house freely, take glasses and crockery off the dresser, maybe even light the stove, settle in? If neighbours saw smoke they would surely infer that something peculiar had happened. Little did she know that neighbours would not see the slightest alteration, even down to the drawing of a blind or the closing of a shutter. Her nearest neighbour was dopey and going blind. The other two cottages were empty and now housed summer folk. Yes, families had gone away, and those that were around whizzed by in motorcars. She was stranded. In her mind, she went up and down the village street and implored every householder and every shop owner to be wise to her plight. He must have left traces somewhere. His fingerprints would be on the gate, unless he wore a stocking or a glove. Since her bedroom door did not lock, she decided at least to take some action to keep him from barging in. She who had been too weak to hobble down the stairs a few days before was now dragging the brown chest of drawers across the floor, stopping sometimes to draw breath or to raise it up when one of the wooden whorls caught in the threadbare carpet. At last. Placing it smack across the doorframe she believed she had at least shown some spunk.

"It's mine . . ."
"It's mine . . ."
"I found it."
"I saw it."

"What in the name of—" Ma Hinchy puts down the pan of ashes she has been emptying, crosses over to the twins, and decides that she has never seen anything so spooky-looking in all her life. Moira tells her how she saw it but couldn't get to it because she couldn't find her other shoe. Maeve got to it. Maeve is jumping up and down now, holding it, swirling it like a duster. The mother dons it and laughs at her image in the mirror, the curved mirror that they use to spot thieves with. She pulls it down over her head clownishly, like a cap, and goes to the shop door to see if anyone will recognise her. A couple of youngsters run off in alarm.

"Oh, a glamour hammer." It's the new young Guard, who has come up for his morning coffee. It's an understanding between them. She helps him, he helps her. A crowd stay in the bar most nights after hours, playing bingo and drinking pints, and it has been agreed that she will be raided only once a year, on a prearranged night when all are religiously drinking glasses of lemonade.

"I took you for someone else," he says.

"Who?"

"Oh, some film star."

"Oh, Donal . . . Donal," she calls to her husband, who is setting out in the tractor, calls to tell him that Guard Flynn took her for a film star. He doesn't answer. He dislikes that Guard, sees no reason to be under a compliment to him. He's off to the bog to collect turf, because the tourists go mad for turf fire and the smell it gives out, have themselves photographed in front of it.

Once placed on the counter the wig looks different. It looks sinister and as if it might move of its own accord. The twins are afraid of it now, neither wanting it, each wanting it to be burned, because it has belonged to a witch. The first customer, who happens to be an educated lady, is asked her opinion of it.

"Miss Cusack, would you mind giving an opinion as to how this thing came to be in our back yard?" Ma Hinchy asks. Miss Cusack has not much to say except to convey her misgivings, says she does not like its aura.

"Aura!" Guard Flynn says, and thinks that because she is a Bachelor of Arts she can fling her gerundives around.

"I reckon it was A *Woman Taken in Adultery*," he says

while picking shavings of coconut from between his teeth and swallowing them.

"Excuse me now, Guard," Ma Hinchy says, pointing to the twins, who are gnawing their thumbs and coveting the biscuits.

"That or theatre folk," he says.

"Unfortunately, we have no theatre folk; the television has destroyed our culture," Miss Cusack says peevishly, as if he were to blame.

"It could be a guy . . . You get guys now dressing up as women."

"Watch your tongue," Ma Hinchy says, and sends the twins to the kitchen to lift the kettle off.

"Transvestites they call them. They look the spitting image of a woman—stockings, suspenders, the lot."

"You have a very outdated notion of women's apparel," Miss Cusack says.

"Would you believe it, I read that a man was married to another man and didn't twig . . . Married and sharing a bed," he says to Ma Hinchy, as if they are privy.

"That's impossible," she says.

"Chinese," he says, and laughs, adding that with their features and fixtures, everything is haywire.

"Maybe I should put a card in the window," Ma Hinchy says, but then concludes that any woman who lost the wig would not want her transgression so shamelessly exposed. With Miss Cusack's help they cite the young girls, the hussies, in the town or in the outskirts who might be the guilty parties.

"I know what," Ma Hinchy says, and going to the open door calls to Colette, the young hairdresser three doors away, to ask if she would please spare a moment on an urgent matter of identification.

Holding it proudly, Colette feels the hair, which she pronounces soft, then with her forefingers measures the depth of the coifs, then studying the lining assures them that it hasn't been worn much. She reckons that it is nun's hair, most probably an Italian nun's, since all the best tresses seem to come from there, and then astonishes them by telling them the approximate price.

"Over a hundred pounds," Guard Flynn says.

"Minimum."

"God in heaven," Ma Hinchy says as the children clamour for a reward.

"So it's not a woman taken in adultery," Miss Cusack says with a piquance.

"Didn't that maniac on the run go into a hairdresser's in Limerick and take a wig?" Colette says.

"Oh feck," Guard Flynn says, but inaudibly, rattled with himself for not having thought of it, and instantly taking hold of the thing, he crushes and recrushes it as if it is an animal that he must restrain.

"You mean the Beast?" Miss Cusack says.

"Good God, and he was in our yard," Ma Hinchy says, opening her dirndl skirt so that her two children can huddle in there like chickens under a mother hen. It is deemed a miracle by her that they are not all pulp, and a greater miracle, considering that her husband was not at home the night before but off in a bus with a lot of women to behold the miracle of a moving statue.

"We could have been murdered in our beds," she says, then looks sharply at Guard Flynn, who is walking off with it.

"State property," he says.

"You can thank Colette for her detective work," Ma Hinchy says.

"I knew all along . . . I knew the minute I set eyes on it," he says, going out, waving it like a trophy.

"Pig," Colette says. She has never liked him, not since the day of the horse show, when he made her park her car half a mile away and walk in her stiletto shoes.

"There are more things, Horatio, in heaven and hell," he says as he strides down the street. This is it. Horatio. Where the hell did he learn that speech? This is it. This is dynamite, baby.

"The cat's meow," he says as he places it on the desk and then moves it in slow menacing little circles, like a ventriloquist.

"What the Christ," the second Guard says, backing off from it.

"Exhibit A, B, C, D . . . What have you?"

"I thought it was a fox."

"A human fox."

"What the hell is it?"

"I was having a stroll up the town . . . I go into Ma Hinchy to get the chocolate biscuits for our coffee and there it is . . . I worked it out in a flash and think to myself, A brand-new wig. I estimate the price, which I later confirm with that nitwit of a hairdresser, and I know . . . I know . . ."

"Whose is it?"

"Whose is it! An item worth over a hundred smackers, abandoned in a back yard, and I say, Would a man wearing this leave it for the birds; would a woman offering her merchandise and caught at it, would she leave such a thing—absolutely not. Would one of those transvestites leave it?"

"What are they, Eamon?"

"Oh, they're half-and-half fellas . . . Never mind them . . . Put your thinking cap on. Who, who?"

"A hippie."

"A hippie, my arse, Tom . . . It's your man . . . It's McGreevy out digging or dumping. It blew off. Think of last night . . . Gale-force winds . . . And think, he fecked a wig, didn't he, in Limerick . . . He was around last night."

"Jesus, we could go out with dogs and get him."

"He can't be far away."

"The hounds would smell him for the animal he is."

"Smell him . . . They'd eat him alive."

"Try it on."

"No . . . I'd hate to . . . It smells."

"How do I look?" Guard Flynn says, donning it and doing a waltz around the room.

"You look like a charwoman," the sergeant says as he comes striding in from the other room. Through the glass divide he had not seen the wig, but now he sees it and sniffs something.

"Take it off . . . Take it off," he says abruptly.

"Kids were playing pooka with it when I found it."

"Put it in a box . . . Label it . . . Write a brief description of how it was found and get it to the forensic office in Dublin."

"That's what I was going to do."

"That's what you were going to do . . . It should reach the forensic office in exactly the condition in which it was found."

"Yes, Sergeant." Always the same, older Guards begrudging you any bit of success. He luxuriates in the plaudits. Brilliant detective work. Superlative skill. Quick in the motion of thought. A father and mother of a coup. The young sleuth hound of Gary-Kennedy. And so on, and so on. Except that, with each shaking, the specks of blue paint disengage and flutter like grains of blue dandruff, then drop harmlessly, weightlessly into the quiet and sedentary dust.

She walks through her several rooms in order to confirm them as hers. A warped and pitiless neglect has invaded every corner, so that there are flaking walls, missing stair rods, stacks of damp and mildewed newspapers, and over a light switch, like some rustic fetish, a tranche of toadstools ripening in the sun. It is morning and she has not slept. A sharpening of the senses has come with his arrival and swarms of memory, even down to her husband, James, writing her that letter at the bureau and overturning the bottle of ink out of spite, that letter telling her to pack her utensils and be gone. Yes, vivid and fluent and harmful like the ink itself dripping off the rosewood onto the floor.

"Good God," she says, seeing the hoar face, her own, in the gilt mirror, a reflection more pitiless than from the clouded hand glass in her bedroom. "Good God," she says it again, and so to the next room, where the bare boards at the far end are strewn with bat turds, like grains of corn, only black, a host of black turds that are without smell. Behind the shutters the bats hang limp in their vigil, still creatures like the brown-black fingers of untenanted gloves, waiting for their true metier, waiting for night. She knows which room he has chosen, her antennae tell her. The room on the ground floor where Paud slept. A single bed, adhesive paper glued to the lower half of the window, pictures of red-breasted robins on it. What does he intend to do with her?

In another room a painting has fallen. Broken glass like a spewed jigsaw rests on a herd of brown bullocks, knee deep in amber waters. The frayed cord hangs from the nail, wispish, a mimicry of the private parts of the faithfully rendered bullocks. At least glass is not a mirror, glass is not nine years' bad luck. There are two hers, the one who does not dare to admit that in Paud's room now there is a dangerous man, a savage, and the other her, which contends that she is mistress of the house. Maybe he is making explosives. She does not know precisely what explosives are, but she well knows what they do and remembers details she has read of, shops, houses, and people blown to crazed insignificances. She recalls someone saying how an explosive was like a piece of cheddar cheese, small, orange in colour, harmless until the device is fitted.

He might blow himself up. She has heard of such things—men in rooms, especially over in London, blowing themselves up by mistake.

In another room the smell of camphor balls issuing from the open door of a painted wardrobe. He opened it when doing his search. James and herself painted that wardrobe in one of their times of reconciliation, first light blue, then dark, the border of flowers having to be drawn with a pencil, her task, a lady's task, as he said. They could not decide whether the flowers were dahlias or asters; they had wide faces and they were a deeper blue, because she put a Reckitts cube in the paint. The blue of grottoes, far-off, fabled places. The smell of camphor lingered, though the little balls themselves had been dissolved by time, sugary motes in the air, seeping into the wood and the hangers that hung lonesome, waiting for use, waiting for drapery.

Should she ask him a question? How long do you intend to stay? What is your object? Do you need towels? Towels! The thought of him washing himself or bathing himself makes her quiver. Washing his crimes away. The last flight of stairs creaks. It always did. It was where James heard the chains, the chains of the dead, and predicted that they were coming for him. Well, they are back now with a vengeance, the chains of history, the restless dead and the restless living, with scores to settle. On the last step she pauses, undecided as to whether to go into the dining room or the drawing room, as if it mattered. Both doors are open, as are the folding baize-covered doors that lead to the morning room. She goes there. Her house seems so precious to her, even its decay. Her house should not have to suffer this.

The sun has made pitter-patterings on the glass top of the cane table, and elsewhere it makes little darting apostrophes. The broken cane of the chair sprouts strands of upstanding stubble. She sees a dog, a red setter, the living image of their

Shep, their favourite dog, the one they both loved and that drew them together as a knowing child draws its sparring parents together, drew them with plaintive looks or the forking or folding of one ear, as if to say, "I'm watching, I'm here." She thinks of her first day as a bride going from room to room, green walls, terra-cotta walls, pictures of mills and millstreams, passages, some dark, some not, and Brid in the kitchen with raised sleeves, laughing and making two kinds of pastry for pies. She thinks of the set of gongs calling people from their rooms, giving calling ladies and gentlemen a summons to hot dinners and largesse, feet on the flagstones, a fiddler brought in to play. One single order from his lot and walls, staircases, gongs and panelling will be no more. He takes her by surprise coming from the back hall carrying an enamel mug and a plastic razor. His T-shirt is short-sleeved and it is as if she is encountering someone naked. What she notices is his colouring, a face bronzed, a tattoo on his wrist, the tricolour, nestling, green, white, and gold, in a circle of indigo. He nods by way of good morning or good day.

"I thought you said there were no animals."

"There are no animals . . . My husband loved horses and bred them," she says in her haughtiest accent.

"I saw a dog," he says.

"Then I didn't dream it," she says, the voice grateful, as if Shep had reincarnated and could be a mascot for her.

"Black dog," he says.

The sun's rays, she now realises, gave the stray animal the mahogany lustre of Shep's coat.

"I saw no black dog," she says.

"You won't be going outside."

"Why not?"

"You haven't been outside . . . so you won't be going outside."

"Is that an order?"

"That's how it is in war."

"It's not my war."

"It's your war whether you like it or not."

"Do you have a name?" she asks with a sting.

"Call me Pat or John or Mick, or whatever you like," he says overcalmly.

"Pat or John or Mick," she says, smarting at his offensiveness.

"Correct." He turns, then retreats down the passage from which he came, obviously too incensed to shave.

"Pup," she says, but not loudly. Her voice is gone. She can feel her left breast against the cup of her brassiere, not like flesh at all, oozy, fear dripping out of her nipple. She knows his face from somewhere, that face is notorious, she can almost put a name to it and a nickname.

He had that sandy pigment that she connected with hoboes and with tinkers. His stubble was sandy and a red colouring moved in stray patches beneath the skin. His moustache was cropped since the morning. He didn't look up when she came in, simply went on with his task, which was the cleaning of a dismantled rifle. The wooden butt on the floor looked exactly like the gauntlet of a leather glove and the rags he was using to clean the barrel she recognised as her own. Dragging the smeared rag out with a long string he looked through the cleaned barrel and laughed at something of his own devising. His eyes were both lively and cruel and had an uncanny ability to stare, to see into her as if she were transparent. He had a chilling authority.

"I wanted a word with you," she said formally.

"Fire ahead."

"Why did you come here . . . why here?"

"The anvil of circumstances."

"I see, or rather I don't see. You intend to talk in riddles."

"Correct." His voice cut. She saw sewing machine oil and an old tin of wax that had gone dry which he was warming on a Primus. Hers. Her dish, her wax, her primus, her house, and yet not hers. A pile of newspapers in the corner seemed to be his day couch, as there was a blanket slung over them and a pillow without a pillow slip. The stained ticking looked shameful to her once-house-proud eyes. How long did he intend staying?

"How long do you intend staying?"

"That depends," he said with the self-same insolence and clippedness.

"You see, it's not very nice at my time of life . . . It's not very convenient," she said, and wished that she had not said "my time of life." He apologised for the inconvenience, said that there weren't many safe houses around, and that surely it was big enough for two.

"Not us two," she said tartly.

The rag stuck in the second barrel and he drew his body and his arm back slowly, as if pulling on an oar. She saw how strong he was and how flexed. Watching without speech she thought, He has a mother or had a mother, he would not kill me, and then realised that in that very tripod of old newspapers possibly lay the evidence of his gruesome deeds. She would rummage through them later on.

"We'll survive." The rag had shredded, and as he picked it out, threadlets stuck to him.

"You forget that you were not invited."

"*O! Bhean an Tighe,*" he said mockingly, then asked if she knew what it meant. Yes, she knew.

"Say it," he said. At first she hesitated, but was forced to say it, forced by the glint in his eyes.

"O! woman of the house," she said, feeling the full and bitter absurdity of it and going out before he could humiliate her more.

In the kitchen she screams. She did not expect to find him there, find him standing by the table eating a piece of bread with something on it, maybe a pickle. She cannot tell in the dark. Their eyes meet each other like two startled animals. Her routine was to go down before five and bring up her tea tray. He had taken the light bulb out of the ceiling in case she had any ideas of going down there later. She had not sat in the kitchen at night for the best part of a year, nor would she now.

"I'm afraid I'm raiding your stocks," he says.

"Help yourself," she says, adding that there was not that much, never at the end of the week before the groceries came. He had already questioned her on that: what she ordered, where they were left, if a person came in or not.

"They're left on the window ledge . . . Two sliced loaves . . . half a pound of cooked ham . . . one pot of jam . . . half a pound of butter . . . A tin of salmon . . . tin of sardines . . . Potatoes and root vegetables . . . Biscuits . . . Rashers . . . The weekly newspaper . . . Cleaning stuff, now and again" was what she said in a scornful singsong voice.

Somehow the dark has given her courage, that and finding him under an obligation to her, so to speak.

"I've been thinking," she says.

"What of?"

"If women ran your organisation there would be no shooting . . . no bombs."

"We have plenty of women."

"Then they're not mothers."

"How would you know whether they're mothers or not?" he says in his cold, impersonal way.

It is too much for her. She says since all is so candid between them, could he tell her in a few simple words what he wants, what his organisation wants, what is the score.

"To get the British out of Ireland."

"And then?"

"Justice for all. Peace. Personal identity. Racial identity."

"We can have that whether we're united or not."

"My people don't have it."

"Your people are not your people . . . Most of them disown you," she says.

"I have friends up and down this country," he says.

It is too much for her. She says if he has friends up and down the country, why not decamp on some of them, why on her, where he is not welcome and where she cannot even strike a match in her own kitchen because of his ruling. She can see not only the glare in his eyes, she can feel the bristle as he puts the bread down and pushes the plate into the centre of the table.

"I'm sure you're a very educated woman, much too educated for me," he says as he goes to the door.

"At least take your supper with you."

"I'm not hungry," he says.

"I hope you don't intend to go on hunger strike," she says. She feels tempted to run after him, to fling it on the floor, to make him grovel.

(JOSIE'S DIARY)

Being in this sort of situation sharpens everything. I notice how cold for instance the frame of my glasses were this morning and I saw each blade of grass outside the window, nodding or still, and the hills so soft and hazed, the near hills and the far, hills that I both loved and hated, spoke to or wept to, the hills as they always were and always will be, soft and genial, the fields with damp on them, a damp that doesn't rise sometimes for the whole day, and the crows in their several excitements swooping and rising to pick the bits of green and clover in between the khaki tufts. I see them all because of this death sentence hanging over me. Maybe I don't have to die. Maybe he'll move on. Or maybe the Guards will get wind of it and rescue me somehow. My fancy keeps imagining a helicopter and a rope coming down to my window and me being hoisted up in some kind of cradle. My fancy imagines that and then imagines something quite other. As for sounds, I tremble at every stir, my kettle coming to the boil or any car or lorry in the distance. I used not to hear them, I used not to hear anything much, now I hear everything except him. He creeps. He is like some sort of wood-animal. Where he trained I don't know. I read somewhere that they train them in Libya. They must creep in Libya. Earlier he did some scrubbing. The sound of the scrubbing brought me down. He was on his knees, half the tiled floor with sudsy water and the other half grimed. The soap was so old that the black lines in it were like ribs of ingrained thread. He scrubbed and scrubbed.

"If my husband were here would you have broken in?" I asked.

"Probably," he said, but did not look up at me. That is what is so macabre, the way he does not show anger or shame or anything. Probably because he has been in gaol or in rented rooms alone, alone, hatching a job.

If I am to die, there is something I want to say, except that I do not know to whom. What I want to say is something about myself. Something deep and difficult about the past and the way I changed, the way we change, get harder, hammer out every bit of softness in us. I think of the rows, rows over money, my husband putting on his cap to go out and escape from me, a black greasy cap that his ire had sweated into, bacon and cabbage, the dogs yelping for the leavings, downpours, and in spite of it all there used to be inside me this river, an expectation for something marvellous. When did I lose it? When did it go? I want before I die to be myself again. Who would think that this impasse would make me say such a thing. It's him. It's death. It stalks like a wolf. I saw on a postcard once how the wolf is at home in the North. That must mean the biting cold, the snow in the gut.

What sound was that? It's like bees, but it's not bees, it can't be, it's the dead of winter. Christmas is four weeks away, Christmas! It is an aeroplane going over, going to America. It passes at the same time every day. Freedom, freedom. When I say the word I can only think of birds, that plummet, that fluidity, the widening wings going up, up, and I think what they would do if they were suddenly made flightless. Sink. Sink.

Sometimes they have priests waiting before they do a job, I know that much. Or the priest may not be got until it's too late. That happened to my poor uncle. His head blown off and yet a part of him asked pardon of God and his mother. I do not want to die like that. I want to die whole. That was the word he expressed about the country. Whole. Wholeness. If I could reason with him all would be different. What I am saying is mad, mad. It comes from no sleep. Neither of us sleeps. I can tell by his eyes, his flinch.

In his quarters, quiet as a monk. She imagines the various things he might be doing. At one moment she thought he was probably making explosives and hoped that by a stroke of good luck he might blow himself up. The next minute she pictured him writing a letter home or looking at the robin redbreasts. Seeing the sun on the grass and on the hills in the distance, seeing the cold winter light, she was seized by a sudden rebellion. Why could she not go out? The nurse has always been telling her that if she walks half a mile a day she will be supple again. Walk. Defy him. As she donned hat and coat she held imaginary conversations with him, and as she slid the bolt back she was sure that she heard him spring from his lair.

She walked over the high grass, using her cane to beat it down, then stood before the tree where her husband's initials were carved, his and his brother's. She remembered how on her wedding day he had marched her out there and showed her the two names, his being the first and the most decisive, the J O M carved into the pinkish trunk, the branches lolling down, the underneath quite dark, a shelter for moulting hens. There were flowers then, yellow flowers and apricot-coloured bushes, but now all was tangled, briars, bushes, and ivy usurping one another in a kind of maul. She looks at the larch trees, she looks at the evergreens, then back at the buried flower beds, and makes absurd and outlandish promises, gardening promises for seasons to come. Where the stone wall is crumbling she vows to have iron stakes put in. Going up the avenue she thinks, Why not make a run for it.

Quickening her pace, she hums loudly, a Fenian song, the only one she knows, about a woman gathering nettles—"Glorio . . . Glorio to the bold Fenian men." Very soon she is winded. Puny her steps, puny the piping intercessions to saints to ask that a farmer or a roadmender go by. The sound of a car in the distance fills her with a piercing sorrow. It might now be turning and heading towards her, speeding and whisking her off to safety, except that it isn't. The sound recedes, and as it does she lifts her hand in a wan wave, like some outcast in a painting waving to a passing ship.

Even as she stands, to inhale the drizzle and the outdoors, she is seeing, feeling, nothing, aware only of the botched and impotent bid for freedom, knowing that presently she is going to retrace her steps, plant her galoshes down in the same rutted footprints, and be answerable to him. The landscape seems alien, sod and grass feel different, his coming has brought menace into the air, his coming the precursor of gruesome deeds.

In the hall he tells her that if she wants to take a wee walk she must wait till night. He is holding binoculars—hers—giving the air of someone used to such fallals.

"Is it a sin to walk?"

"You said you hadn't been out for months."

"Well, I was out now," she says, and throwing caution to the wind as she might throw tea leaves, she tells him that she knows who he is, remembers gun battles, his death missions, his daredevil escapes, his ability to be invisible, and yes, his nickname.

"I've never targeted a civilian," he says.

"I suppose I'll be the first," she says.

"I hope you're not," he says, gallingly calm.

"Oh, brave soldier," she says, gloating in the sarcasm, careless now of what he might do, possessed briefly of the brazen and garrulous temper that was hers as a young girl. She will show him, she will best him somehow.

She sat in her room. She did not come out in answer to his knock and then in answer to his call. She could hear him come up and knew that probably he had left a cup of tea outside. She sat looking at the evening sky that was at once so placid and so inviting, at the trees without leaves, silhouetted against that sky and other trees in the distance, purple, the purple of the hills, and she imagined the lake dark and choppy, but she could not see it. She envisaged the churchyard where her husband was and the space next to him which awaited her, the plot under the tall tomb where his forebears lay. The tall tomb stark with lichen, white lichen, beautiful but stark in the evening light. Yes, he had probably left tea outside. He was quiet. All was quiet. She believed that if she sat still some miracle would happen.

And so she prayed. She prayed kneeling, standing, walking about. Sometimes her hands pummelled each other and sometimes she ran her fingers carefully over each bead of her rosary. She kissed the crucifix. She said prayers she knew and prayers she did not know, childhood prayers and impromptu ones. She prayed to the Sacred Heart and all the saints in heaven.

(A VOLUNTEER'S DIARY)

23rd January 1921. Slept in a dugout. The sides of the dugout were built with stones and clay and thatched with rushes. It measured about nine feet by seven. It had to accommodate eight men. In this abode we spent many a hard winter night with a leaky roof and a wet bed. The door consisted of a furze bush.

29th January. Constructed a new residence, a cowshed belonging to M. Sammon. Into this three of us brought a bed and were fairly comfortable, although the wall was airy and the roof faulty. In this abode we stopped for about a month, spending an occasional night on the mountain when things got too hot. One night a step came to our door—we immediately got our revolvers, thinking we were surrounded, but it turned out to be a donkey eating the hay we had stuffed in the holes.

February. Started with C. Turner to go to a wedding near Loughrea and ran into a cycling patrol near Woodford, but they did not know us and we got safely through. Cycled home from wedding and escaped military by a neck in Mount Shannon.

8th March. Received orders to report for an attack on a patrol in Feakle. Proceeded in company with T. Mack and Ernie and J. Mack to Aughrim, where we spent that night. Raining torrents. At night we proceeded to Feakle and took up positions and remained in the town for about two hours. The 'Tans scented danger and remained indoors. We then sniped the barrack, and heavy firing and bombing came from the barrack for about two hours. They continued firing after we were gone. Home, very wet at 1:00 a.m. and slept at M. Walsh's.

March. Slept next night at Cleary's.

March. Heard that three men with strange accents were looking for me. They were near me several times during the day but we did not meet. My suspicions became aroused so I proceeded across the mountain believing them to be auxiliaries. Eight of us met up and proceeded to search the district where they were likely to have stopped. We came through the mountain and down the pass onto Costello's Cross—seven in number we divided our party, three stopping in Burke's hayshed while four of us lay in wait around the barn where we thought they would stop. It was freezing hard and I had fallen into a drain early in the night so that after four hours I was frozen stiff. At 2:00 a.m., thinking they might be inside, we searched barn but found only where they had slept in the hay. As we went back to the men, we saw signalling with a lamp about half a mile away. We now concluded that they had seen us and were signalling to Killaloe for reinforcements so we proceeded home. Next day they came from Killaloe and burned the barn and arrested two men where we had delayed near the cross the previous night. Four of them were waiting inside the fence expecting to get the remainder of us, but we had gone to Whitegate. If we had not got information about the two men they arrested they would have shot the lot of us, as we had only one revolver and a .38 on us.

March. Slept in dugout in Derrycon. Used to leave every morning about 5:00 a.m. and cross to Bohatch Mountain about two miles away, where we would stop until 10:00 a.m., and return to the lowlands for breakfast when we knew there was no enemy about. The weather at this period was very severe with snow and rain and we suffered much from exposure in consequence.

April. The long expected roundup came at last. Derrycon and Bohatch were not taken in, but Sammons, which we vacated a few days previously, was discovered.

5th April. We decided to erect a new hut in Bohatch Mountain and set to work accordingly and had it finished soon. It was a dugout in the side of a hill and roofed with sheet iron over which was heath sods. This hut was used only for a fortnight and was very wet and cold. It was situated about a mile from the road, and going in in the dark you fell into a few bog holes.

This dugout seems to have been spied upon and I narrowly escaped being captured, not being there on the morning they came.

12th April. Got orders to join flying column. Eight of us started from Middleline Cross at 5:00 a.m. and joined column at Aughrim, where we spent that night.

17th April. Heard Mass at Clunta and then marched to a secret place where we waited all day expecting a patrol from Tullagh. We left the position about 4:00 p.m. and marched to Cahir, arriving at 1:00 a.m. That evening we resumed march again and arrived at Scalp Mountain, where we billeted for the night.

April. We are on the move again and marched across the mountain to Derrybrien, where we spent the night. Next day arrived at Dalystown expecting enemy. We were only there a short while when the 'Tans arrived to surround the position. Our ammunition supply was too small for a long-distance fight so we did not engage them and resumed our march after they had gone.

May. Back to the Scalp Mountains twenty-five miles away . . .

"A good man . . . who was he?" he said as he looked up. In his eyes she felt a yield; something in the diary had touched him, corresponded with his own journeying.

"He was shot by the Black and Tans . . . They found him and his comrades that next day . . . They were in a vacated house sleeping . . . The caretaker was outside keeping watch and putting down cabbages. He wouldn't give them away . . . He was arrested along with them . . . They were all brought in a lorry, brought down to a bridge in a town and shot. There is a song about it . . ."

"There's a song about it," he says, and riffles the pages of the curled-up worn diary as if it is a pack of playing cards.

"So I do know."

"What do you know?" he asks.

"History . . . Our woes."

"Your uncle was one of us?"

"I was in America working . . . I didn't even know that he had died . . . Yet he stood at the end of my bed and called me home."

For some reason she softens, the thought of her uncle shot so callously, of his last words to the priest, which her mother had sent her, and she remembers how she read them and how she wept and thought of home, the small roads, the hawthorn hedges, her uncle so quiet and grave and abstinent, her uncle shot dead, and how she thought it was wrong, wrong, and how she should come home and help to put it right. Yes, those sentiments had risen up in her then and were still there like spores lurking.

"Why did you show me this?" he asks.

"So's you'd know."

"Know what?"

"That we are on the same side."

"Are we?"

"Except that what they did then was different."

"It wasn't . . . It's exactly the same."

". . . Innocent people."

"For Christ's sake, I'm trying to save my fucking country, so stop telling me about innocent people."

"Then fucking do it . . . Without having to kill and maim innocent people," she says, shocked at her own directness.

"Look, missus . . . You stick to your gracious living and your folklore."

"Are you afraid of me?" she asks, and allows a smile.

"Why should I be afraid of you—you?"

"Afraid of what I might say."

"Talk has got us fucking nowhere in our fight."

"Maybe you don't want it to."

"Look . . . you would have to be born there to know it," he says, and with a coldness he hands her back the diary, meaning that she has been wasting her time and his.

(JOSIE'S DIARY)

He went out last night after dark. To discuss a job. They don't call it death or murder, they call it a job. This house will be notorious for the fact that he hid here. There will be exaggerations. How I was chained or put under the stairs, bits of me cut off. They won't know the truth. The truth always gets lost, big truths, small truths, no matter what. Lost. I wonder what he does all day. Does he read? Rehearse what he is going to do? Maybe he's one of these people who daydream. He doesn't eat much. He ate only one slice of the two slices of bread and ham that I left out for him. Why did I do it? I don't know why. The grocery order had come and the ham looked fresh and I thought

—well, I thought. For some reason they sent candles with the groceries and that made me wonder. Anyhow, I made him a nice sandwich. Same thing when I came on him in the larder. It was near dusk. He was cleaning his boots. He put his hand up to switch on the light, but I knew there were mushrooms there, a mildewed crop all bundled together, and I knew he'd get electrocuted.

"Don't," I shouted, and told him why.

"Thanks," he said, but without any sentiment. He did not turn on the light. Maybe I thought it would bring us closer.

When things get down to brass tacks, everything looks very final and very raw. Death is everywhere now. It rattles like jugs. If I could tell him that, if I could tell him how simple, how dreadful, the nearness of death is to me now, he might pity me. He has a mother. He has a sister. He must know a woman's feelings, how she wants to give life, not to take it. If he saw me sitting counting my own short breaths, some sort of sea change would occur in him, or would it? The way they train them is probably macabre. To be invincible. No chinks. Out in isolated places shooting targets, reading up, mettling themselves, taking the oath. Once they cross that divide they're never the same again, like iron put into a fire. They cannot return to their old shape or their old ways. The saddest bit is that we're the same stock, the same faith, we speak the same tongue and yet we don't. Language to each of us is a Braille that the other cannot know. Words like justice or love or bread turned inside out or outside in. Nothing escapes him. I threw an old toffee paper out the window and a dried-up box of rouge. He asked if it was a signal of some kind. I said no. He said one cannot be too vigilant. I said I wasn't answerable for what I did anymore and he looked at me with the first, the very first, twinge of pity. It was probably my hair, it was streeling down.

"If you walk on that wet paint I'll kill you," Jakko says.

"Yap yap yap," Nellie the dog says by way of self-congratulation, seeing she has swum over and is dripping from every particle of herself, sniffing, approving maybe the smell of paint, but not the sour ammonia smell of the glue pasting the wallpaper. The strips of wallpaper drying are like bits of tripe.

"I said I'd kill you," he says, his eyes scanning her dainty little footprints, which are like quill marks, as she explores the deck, the berths, and then bounces on the cream-coloured cushions.

"I'll tie a stone around your neck and drown you . . . That's what I'll do." She knows what he is saying, and by her little cheeky gait and her thin bickery tongue she is saying back to him, "You can't kill me, I'm all you have, Jakko Mulcahy."

It's his smoke time. Twice a day, eleven in the morning and four in the afternoon, he sits in front of the stove in the saloon and smokes his pipe. He's been asked to light the stove and get the cruiser well heated. He'd stay forever. The peace and quiet of it, the birds, the motions of the water. Two more days to go. A coat of varnish on the inside and a second coat of gloss all round. He'd love to take off in her then, him and Nellie, across the lake and up the lordly Shannon, the Pilgrim's Way, a thing he'd always wanted to do, go through the big locks and the swing bridges, find a mooring at dusk, up to the town to a pub, wakening to the breath of nature, the herons, the grebe, and the mute swan, all around the hills bestirring themselves, heaving up out of the plains, blue and lilac, hills magnifying into mountains.

No wonder the Englishman loves it. Has been coming for thirty years, but missed out for the last few years on account of nasty incidents. Homesick for the place although it is not his home. Orders sent on ahead to give it a complete overhaul: the engine, the roof, the rails, to air it thoroughly because of the Englishman not being at all well. His not being at all well was conveyed by Miss Hourigan in low insinuating tones, as if he had a serious illness, cancer or something like that. Cancer getting its grip on everyone as it had on his wife.

"Spick-and-span, Jakko," Miss Hourigan said, and gave him a list that covered two full pages. Sir Roland's secretary had phoned and read out the things, stressing that it must be warm and that the bunks must be aired, hot-water bottles put in the bunks twice a day so that the party would not catch pneumonia. Four men. No ladies. Dinner in the hotel their first night. Had requested a regional menu—fresh oysters, suckling pig with potatoes and cabbage, and Miss Hourigan's lemon meringue pie.

"He's been coming for thirty years . . . Our oldest VIP . . . And I'm glad that he's decided to come back to us," Miss Hourigan said.

"I know," Jakko said, and remembers being gillie to Sir Roland, remembers how testy he was if other boats came in on his patch and the debate one evening as to what name to call the cruiser, his wife wanting an Irish name and Sir Roland wanting his wife's name and in the end their settling for a made-up name—*Serendipity*. No one knew what it meant. He remembers that Sir Roland always called him Paddy, even though his name was Jakko, and shouted at him once when he asked him a simple question, a point of law, Sir Roland himself being a notable judge. *Serendipity*. The name had faded, but with a little sable brush he gave it definition again, brought it back to the cheeky duck-egg blue it had been—*Serendipity*.

"And you behave yourself," he says to Nellie, who is fiddling with the pompoms of a knitted scarf. He'll put up a sign that says WET PAINT to keep them out. He'd sleep there overnight but for Miss Hourigan, she'd say he was taking advantage. Heaven to sit in front of the stove in the nicely varnished room and smoke and watch the dark coming on, that nice queer sensation of dark coming over water, creeping over it, and the mountains getting dark too and bulky, and he'd imagine all sorts of things, that it was his boat, his own boat, which his daughter in America had paid for, and he'd sneak out to the town and get two pints of stout and a sausage roll and throw one of the mattresses down by the warm stove, warmer than his own bloody house with buckets to catch the downpours.

"Wouldn't it be just gorgeous," he said to Nellie, who is on her hind legs looking up at him with her wet, mauvish, pernickety snout.

"Where did you get that thing?" he says, and pulls either end of the scarf and drags her towards him, her little narrow face and her little felt ear pure thoroughbred, and the rest of her a bit of everything.

"You've more than one father," he says, and laughs. He'd bring her on the cruise. She'd be guard dog against hoboes and courting couples. How many had dossed in it since it was last used? He smelt cigarettes the first day. How many couples had lain there, caroused of a night? Too mean to pay him a steady wage, to make him caretaker, watching it, keeping an eye out at all times. Too mean by far. People living in London in one house five nights a week, then off for weekends to an estate in Staffordshire, Spain to a summer residence, and all the while their little white water bus lonely and deserted, rusting in a boathouse, at the edge of the choppy water.

"Maybe he'll leave it to me in his will," he says, laughing at Nellie because with the scarf tied under her chin she resembles an old granny.

"Ask me if I had a good life, Nellie." She almost does. She tips him with her paw, tenderly, daintily, knowing.

"Don't ask me," he says then, and takes out the little notebook in which he is to docket his expenses and wonders how much overtime he can fiddle.

We learn that it was at the bidding of an angel that St. Calum, came to Inis Cealtra with his followers. He found there a tree by name Tilia whose juice distilling filled a vessel and that liquor had the flavour of honey and the headiness of wine. Calum lived in Inis Cealtra for a long time, and the birds of heaven were wont to have friendly intercourse with him and to sport fluttering about his face. He died of the pestilence known as Crom Chonai.

St. Caimin later became Abbot and he was of a mother who had numerous children. His half brother was Guaire Aidne (the Hospitable), legendary King of Connaught and St. Colman of Kilmacduagh fame. There is a well-known tale which is found in the twelfth century Book of the Dun Cow *concerning St. Caimin and his half brothers.*

The three men met in the church of Holy Island and there discussed what each of them would wish to see the church filled with. Guaire wished it to be filled with gold and silver so that he might show generosity to the poor. Cuimmine Fota wished it to be filled with books so that students might learn from them the way of truth. Caimin wished the church to be filled with every kind of disease and sickness, so that all these diseases might be inflicted on his own body.

Caimin's wish seems to have been granted, for all kinds of disease and sickness were inflicted on his body—"so that no bone of him joined another bone on the earth, but they melted and decayed with the anguish of every disease and every tribulation."

Another picturesque tale associated with him may be read in Keating. A nun came to Diarmait, the King of Ireland, to complain that Guaire Aidne had taken from her her only cow. Diarmait assembled an army to avenge this wrong; and though he had but a small army and Guaire a numerous following, the Connaught men were defeated because St. Caimin took the side of Diarmait and "fasted on" Guaire, that he should not be successful in battle.

Just as she overhears him in his quarters, walking, flexing, doing his exercises, she too is determined to keep her wits, to move the joints of fingers and toes and to read aloud so as to confound him. He stands in the doorway, hesitant, then asks if the island she is reading of is the one seen from the shore.

"You've been down to the lake."

"I had a stroll."

"Good," she says, as if to a dutiful tourist.

He has been twice in the middle of the night and will again, dry runs to go through the motions, mentally finishing the job.

"You should see it in summertime," she says, and conjures up the fanciful picture of a waterway winged with bright sails. His silence perhaps it is that makes her gabble on about the dapping season, her husband's renown with the rod, knowing where the trout fed, how to throw, how to make them take, how to play them, how to land them, and then in a welter of excitement she describes the big fish, the biggest fish ever caught on the lake, caught by her husband and sent to Dublin to a taxidermist and then put in a glass case in a hotel. The sweet and arch reminiscences of a woman wishing she was conversing with an ordinary young man.

"They say fishing is very good for you," he says.

"You should try it," she says, and the smile that he returns is one of bemusement.

"Do you want to see something?" and before he can reply, she is up, the tartan rug trailing off her knees, and she is down the hall in search of something. From under the stairs she takes out a biscuit tin, the painted ornamental paper yellowed from time and gauzed in cobweb. It contains her husband's fishing tackle, every single item neatly and scrupulously placed like a child's arrangement of chosen toys. She explains each thing: the feathered bait, which one for which, which hook, which line, and then holding up a mallet of iron she says, "Guess what this is called," and answers, "A priest."

"A priest!" he says.

"Yes, to hit the fish on the back of the pole and conk him out." And together they laugh and wonder why it should be called a priest.

Two people in a freezing house, a couple of night-storage heaters, the smell of must, but with it, in her reveries the remaindered smells of wax polish and big tea roses, the grandeur in beams and arches, the glitter from the blue-green glass chandelier, the lavish suppers—two people united by the sentiment contained in a tackle box, the feathers fresh and jaunty as if just plucked from a pheasant or a rooster, two people bound for a moment in that caesura of winter light, warmed by each other's company, each other's breath.

"I'll tell you what . . . It's more a thing for a man than a woman," she says, and thrusts the tin into his hands with something akin to joy. So long since she has given anyone anything, since she has had the opportunity to. He says she will miss it, surely. She insists. Everything happens then; his eyes grateful and shy, like magnets brushed with gold, and something soft and yielding in her bearing, as if drenched in moonlight.

"It's too much."

"It's yours," she says, and holds it until he takes it and mutters some sort of embarrassed thanks. Everything happens then.

"Yes, the lake is our pride . . . It made us illustrious . . . People came here . . . strangers . . . All sorts of people," she says.

"What do people fish for in winter?" he asks.

"Now! My goodness . . . The waves get as high as the mountains. Small boats would crash on the rocks . . . We lost two young men last year . . . The search went on for days . . . dragging the bottom with hooks." And then her voice grows grave. "The bodies are always found standing up, standing at the bottom of the water like ghouls."

"Like ghouls," he says.

"Yes, and who looks at them are the locals—the men," she says, piteous tears welling up in her eyes. But he has moved away. He came to this house not to feel, not to listen, not to fall into the trap of being wooed, and his eyes now are like blobs of rain rusted upon.

"Last seen . . . last seen . . . Mickey Mouse stuff," Detective Horan says as he sits in his office stuffing pieces of cut paper into his mouth. It is what he does when he is on edge. His family and friends put it down to many things, being weaned too early or being given pieces of paper in preparation for his first Holy Communion. He puts it down to frustration, getting nowhere, this tearaway making apes of them all, even to the extent of stripping a young policeman of his uniform and wearing it for a good thirty miles of his trip south.

"What else does she say?" he asks; he has to shout because of a bad line.

"Only what I told you."

"Repeat what you told me," he says. The young man's stammer is unfortunate.

It takes a full five minutes to impart—how it was in a cinema in Dundalk, no more than twenty people in the audience, the main picture not started, and a fellow came in with a bag, changed his shirt and his vest, and hopped it a few minutes later, leaving behind one of the shopping bags.

"Where is it?"

"A cleaner dumped it."

"Dumped it . . . Thought nothing of it . . . So why is it information now?"

"The usherette seen a photograph of this fellow on television and twigged."

"Twigged what?"

"That it was him or his spitting image."

"What! Curly hair, square chin, high cheekbones, or straight hair, round chin, and no cheekbones—more people have seen this bloke than have seen Our Lady of Fatima."

"Is that a fact."

"No, Vincent, that's not a fucking fact . . . A fact, in the lines of enquiry, would be, where is the bag."

"They're tracing it in the dump."

"How did this 'suspect' speak?"

"Sort of nice, she said. He said to her, 'How you doin?' "

"They all fucking say that."

"There was one other thing . . . A receipt fell out of the bag and they found it under the carpet."

"Oh, cheers—exhibit A. Have you sent it?"

"I'm going to."

"It might be dozy up there in Monaghan, but down here in the collating room in Phoenix Park, my job is on heat, and while we're at it, 'Evidence is always there, Pat . . . Whether it is found is another matter. That it is not found does not prove its absence,' and will you get off my fucking hot line *now*."

"She recognised his smile from that photograph on television."

"He is not smiling in that photograph on television . . . He is cursing and blinding two Guards who had him handcuffed as he was led away from court. Moreover, that was five years ago and he had hair on his head."

"She's sure it's him, anyhow."

"Tell her she can have him with sugar up the Dublin mountains if she's a bit more ginned up," he says, hangs up, then spits out the pile of grey-white matter that his saliva has puttied into a ball.

"It was never a lucky house," she said.

"In what way?"

"Every way."

"My husband used to hear chains on the stairs at night," she said, reliving it, listening, then repeating it as nearly as possible in James's voice. No, she could not say whose chains they were or who was chained, all she could say was that they were to be heard on the stairs going clank-clank and prevented sleep.

"The dead," she said.

"More likely the living," he said. They were having their tea together, half the scrubbed table covered with newspaper and then a cloth, the nice cups with splashes of maroon. He said that since they were in the same house they might as well sup together. He had got the electric oven working and would make bread later on when the milk got sour.

"I can buy extra bread," she said. Again the look. He did not have to say it, she realised for herself; she was not to change her weekly grocery order by even one packet of biscuits. The same things each week, no more, no less.

"What if I get sick?" she said, a sudden revolt starting up in her, a sense of injustice.

"I hope you don't," he said almost chivalrously.

"I have high blood pressure," she said, asking if by any chance he had observed the patches of colour that sometimes appeared on her neck and her cheeks.

"Does the doctor come?"

"He comes on Sundays after Second Mass."

"When you send for him?"

"He comes," she said. It was her first lie and he knew it. The truth was, the doctor came when the notion struck him; he might come at Christmas, or in the summer, or if he was passing. He was a new doctor, young, opinionated, and he rode horses on Sundays. For her visitor he would have no time. Like most people he called them thugs, sickos, and said if the country were to be united in the morning he and his kind would be criminals out of a job. The doctor had described to her once after a bank robbery having to tend to a young pregnant assistant who was losing her child, and how it was the saddest thing on earth to hear her recite the names she had picked, boys' names and girls' names, names that she loved.

"Psychopaths," he had called them. Well, there was one in her kitchen, her spick-and-span kitchen, which he had cleaned. Delft and jugs that he had washed were on the draining board and the windows had miniature rainbows in them where he had shone them.

"What's his name?" he asked.

"D'Arcy," she said, and repeated it as if he didn't believe her.

"You say he comes Sundays," he said, looking at her carefully.

"The odd Sunday," she said, and looked into her teacup, wondering what the glut of tea leaves might portend.

"You don't read cups by any chance?" He smiled. He said no, that that particular little talent had escaped him, although he knew someone who did and who told his mother she would have seven sons, and she did.

"I suppose you don't communicate with her."

"I love my mother," he said, and it was the first time she saw him smile. Yes, it was a real smile, there was no artifice in it.

"But . . . she can't . . . love you."

"I think . . . she does," he said, and brought his hands to his face to hide whatever emotion he was determined to hide. Through those hands, pink from water and suds, he said he hated to upset his mother, to cause her suffering of any kind.

Things she has read keep coming back to her, particular murders, in fields, or on roadsides, priests brought to give extreme unction to the dead and dying, then next day more murders, retaliation from one crowd to another, then some couple in a lonely cottage gunned down at dawn, then a supermarket, and on and on. She remembers being at a funeral and how someone had said that both lots should be put in a stadium and made to shoot one another in rotation, a prolonged blitz until they were a heap of carnage, twined and twisted together like the innocents they had killed, and how a distraught woman had stood up and in a croaking voice said, "You've forgotten your country's wrongs," whereupon people had moved away from her, realising that she was a sympathiser. Hard to think that he had spilt blood. How much blood had he spilt, how many deaths had he caused, and were they in daylight or under cover of dark, and as he walked away or ran away what did he think and how many rifles did he have hidden down in his room?

"When you shoot, which part do you aim for?" she asked.

"The biggest part," he said, and felt his chest with his hand, either in imitation of shooting or being shot at. She froze. There was no tremor in his voice, no inconclusiveness, simply the reply, shooting the biggest part, like shooting a wall.

(JOSIE'S DIARY)

I see him all the time, particularly his eyes. They are amberish with specks of green in them. The colour of the tobacco he rolls. The picture of him tossing the match into the corner re-

minded me of men at home, men I barely knew who came in at night to smoke. They tossed matches everywhere. Somehow when he did it I felt the same sort of bonhomie. How do I know that word? I know words now that I usedn't to know. We meet in the morning room to get a bit of sun. My idea. A million ghosts sit there, including the dapping people who came, the husbands and wives and my own husband, who was cut out to be a gentleman. He says he is glad we talk. He says he loves truth, he loves justice, he loves children. He sings whenever he dandles a baby. What babies has he dandled? He washes before he sees me. He washes strenuously, so that what I notice is the fresh pink of his hands and of his face, washed and rewashed. Is he washing away blood? Is he washing away shame? He is not ashamed. He says it is a war, a war. Him in uniform and the others in uniform. What I would like is for him to be him and at the same time not him. I like everything about him except what he does. When he talks he says nothing excessive. It is as if the years and years of whatever have honed him down or maybe hardened him or both.

He opened a large bottle of orangeade, a treat for us both. He must have got it when he went out, that and the cigarettes. Who does he see? Where does he go? I thought I knew this part of the country. I thought I knew the people up in the village and every house around, but I don't. All is confusion. I asked rather tentatively if others would be coming and he said with all the deference in the world that he would be solo, as he believed it was what I most wanted, I did not want my house turned into a barracks. We drank the orangeade slowly, so slowly. I found it immensely sweet and thick and he saw that I did not like it. He took out a worn piece of paper on which he had written three things. It was in answer to some questions of mine. Justice. Personal identity. Truth. He was looking to see if I understood or if I objected. The handwriting was quite poor. He wants my admiration, he wants my trust. He wants my ca-

maraderie. He says he even wants my happiness. When I had difficulty sitting down he said, "Do you have an onion?" Onion water, he said, was the best thing for rheumatism. He knew that from people at home. What people at home? To think that fields away, or certainly a few main roads away, there are people to whom his name represents the most vile and violent psychopath. Fear he has none. He says he gave up fear long, long ago, that is if he ever had it. He also gave up the Catholic faith. He made his first Holy Communion, he and his brothers and sisters. He misses them. He misses home, the solidarity, the countryside. He believes that one day there will be peace. It is like a flame inside his head. It is in his eyes and in his smile, a sort of radiance. I know now how people have followers, how they draw others to themselves like shining magnets. Maybe he is mad. Maybe that is the secret of him.

Funny, I dreamt of him. A little gold sleeper that he was trying to put through my ear, except that the hole had sealed up. It wouldn't go through. He licked the tip, then started to pierce it through. A sudden warm ejaculation of blood and his saying, "I know I'm hurting . . . but it's for a good reason . . . It's for the nicest possible reason."

If he were to touch me, shake my hand for instance, I would jump. But he won't touch me. He is decorousness itself, the way he reached down for it when my shawl slipped, the way he draws his hands up under his short sleeves and asks if I am all right or if I have slept well. He brought cushions for the cane chairs, found them in another room and aired them on the stone hot-water bottle that he found in the pantry.

It is hard to get him to talk. For instance with Christmas not far off I asked if he would be going home. He smiled. Apropos of nothing he said that when he was a youngster and came South he thought everything was better—the weather, the lemonade, the holly berries.

"And now?" I said.

"The South forgot us," he said. Forlorn. Aggrieved. A likeness to those children in fable, banished again and again, exiled in lakes for hundreds of years, cut off from the homeland.

"Now there are two wars . . . one with the English and one with ourselves," I said.

"Sadly," and then, in a more civil voice, he mentioned that he had liked me from the very start, had an intuition about me, that I was a good woman.

The only thing of beauty in the morning room is an oil lamp on its Corinth base. The bowl has oil in it, oil the colour of red currants and viscous like gum. A beautiful tinted shade enfolds the long, thin globe. A thing of beauty, rose red at the base, then fading to a near transparency, and then at the top fluting to a wavy red-rose border. I pointed to it, said there was a drop of oil left, and it could be lit. He apologised, said he was sorry for all the various embargoes, the rules, said then that he hated that day when he tackled me about the walk, because of course I needed fresh air, it's only natural. I asked if there were moments in his life when he panicked. He thought about it and looked away, looked out the window at a purple bush that was wobbling in the wind and said yes, yes. He could not tell me until we got to know one another better. This could go on for months or a year. Yet I feel it is a matter of days. I have intuitions, just like he has.

"Aoife, tell your daddy . . . Tell your daddy what you told me . . . Aoife."

Aoife cannot speak. She feels as if she has no tongue at all, it's slipped back down into her gullet where the sweets go. She's promised a sweet when she tells. Her mother has already heard it, in fits and starts: how she got home from school, got the key from under the rain barrel, let herself in, and while she was eating a biscuit the red man ran under the wall outside the kitchen window. Her mother heard how she hid and then peeped out and he was around the corner, nearly naked, washing himself in the rain barrel and, seeing her, said he was starving, he'd eat a young child.

"Tell your daddy, Aoife," Sheila says, and begins to reinvent the gruesome caller, his grinning, his naked chest, his splashing in their rain barrel and how it will have to be emptied presently. Rory is taking his little girl's pulse and telling her to stop blinking and look at her daddy.

"It's easy seeing that she's not afraid of you," his wife says, and pulls Aoife off his lap.

"It wasn't me . . . It was Nancy," Aoife says down into her shoes.

"Aoife," her mother says, and starts to shake her shoulders violently.

"We both saw him . . . He was washing his feet in the river . . . The red man that was on the television, with the moustache."

"Put your tongue out, Aoife," Rory says.

"I have no tongue," she says.

"Are you telling the truth?" he asks, and reaches for her to come on his knee again.

"Nancy saw him and she told me." But the tears are already engulfing her, and even though it is wrong and she gets a slap for it from her mother, she goes to her daddy and cries on his good uniform and says all the girls in her class say that the red man will kidnap them. Having said the word she now revels in the sound of it. Kid-nap. Kid-nap. Kid-nap. She starts to have her fits, so that every bit of her trembles and her daddy has to hold her and carry her to the bedroom and place her down on the big eiderdown that is the colour of roses and read her the story she loves . . .

One Sunday morning, after the other two had gone to Mass, the old henwife came into the kitchen to Trembling and said, "It's at church you ought to be this day, instead of working here at home."

"How could I go?" said Trembling. "I have no clothes good enough to wear at church, and if my sisters were to see me there, they'd kill me for going out of the house."

"I'll give you," said the henwife, "a finer dress than either of them has ever seen. And now tell me what dress will you have?"

"I'll have," said Trembling, "a dress as white as snow, and green shoes for my feet."

Then the henwife put on the cloak of darkness, clipped a piece from the old clothes the young woman had on, and asked for the whitest robes in the world and the most beautiful that could be found, and a pair of green shoes.

That moment she had the robe and the shoes, and she brought them to Trembling, who put them on. When Trembling was dressed and ready, the henwife said: "I have a honey bird here to sit on your right shoulder, and a honeysuckle flower to put on your left. At the door stands a milk-white mare, with a golden saddle for you to sit on and a golden bridle to hold in your hand."

Trembling sat on the golden saddle; and when she was ready to start, the henwife said: "You must not go inside the door of the church, and the minute the people rise up at the end of Mass, do you make off and ride home as fast as the mare will carry you."

When Trembling came to the door of the church there was no one inside who could get a glimpse of her but was striving to know who she was; and when they saw her hurrying away at the end of Mass, they ran out to overtake her. But no use in their running; she was away before any man could come near her. From the minute she left the church till she got home, she overtook the wind before her, and outstripped the wind behind.

She came down at the door, went in, and found the henwife had dinner ready. She put off the white robes and had on her old dress in a twinkling.

When the two sisters came home the henwife asked: "Have you any news today from the church?"

"We have great news," said they. "We saw a wonderful grand lady at the church door. The like of the robes she had we have never seen on woman before. It's little that was thought of our dresses beside what she had on; and there wasn't a man at the church, from the King to the beggar, but was trying to get a look at her and know who she was."

The sisters would give no peace till they had two dresses like the robes of the strange lady; but honey birds and honeysuckles were not to be found.

Next Sunday the two sisters went to church again and left the youngest at home to cook the dinner.

After they had gone, the henwife came in and asked: "Will you go to church today?"

"I would go," said Trembling, "if I could get the going."

"What robe will you wear?" asked the henwife.

"The finest black satin that can be found, and red shoes for my feet."

"What colour do you want the mare to be?"

"I want her to be so black and so glossy that I can see myself in her body."

"And what do I see in Aoife's stomach?" her daddy asks, putting the book aside.

"An orange."

"And."

"Weetabix."

"And."

"Smarties."

"And. And. And."

"If you catch him he'll shoot you."

"No, he won't . . . I have the hen mother and I have Aoife and I have honeysuckle and a honey bird . . ."

Again she gives in to the fits, both because she is afraid and because there is something lovely about being held, held.

"I'm well able for that lad," he says, and thinks that if only these criminals were tried not by grownups, but by children, they'd come in with their heads shaven and their hands up and the arms dumps would open of their own accord and the weapons would walk all over the land, like the dead in the famine times, walking to the mass graves.

"Who's that?" she asks, making her way down the stairs to the hall door. All who know her realise that it is to the back door they must come and ring the cowbell that hangs on a bit of blue rope. If it is a tinker, as she believes it will be, she is resolved to hear no rigmarole about starving children and the freezing cold. She knows too that he is lurking somewhere, poised to discover who it is. As she opens the door slowly and drags it back on its sill, a consignment of leaves scurries into the hall.

At first she does not recognise the figure with the knitted cap pulled down over his face, and for a moment she thinks it is a detective, but the barking voice is one she has known all her married life and one that she dreads—the Snooper.

"Martin," she says.

"Your phone is up the spout," he says.

Quickly, without even having to think, she says that she was going to report it but that she had a touch of flu.

"Oh, it's going around," he says, and adds that she looks shook. By the way he stands, it is clear that he is expecting to be brought in. She has never liked him. She knows why she has never liked him. He was present for every single humiliation of hers, always snooping, always there.

"I'd ask you in, only I'm poorly and the house is freezing," she says.

"Ah sure, I have coats on," he says, and takes a step in anyhow, and in that gesture she suspects something more.

"Did you come about the phone?" she says.

"The phone and to see how you were," he says, he who put it about what a hypocrite she was, crying at her husband's graveside, crying and stumbling when she had been the one to drive the poor man mad.

"Why aren't you at work, Martin?" she says crisply.

"Work! I chucked that," he says, and adds that he has the life of Riley, walking roads, going down to the lake and back, popping into the graveyard, meeting people old and new. He mentions a family who have come, a family of hippies with several children, the man's children and the woman's children, the man being one nationality and the woman another. He mentions that they make their own bread and that they brew their own beer. He mentions that they are always looking for empty bottles, empty water bottles and empty wine bottles to distill the beer into. He mentions a gaily-coloured wooden toy hanging from the ceiling that revolves, a carousel, for the children to be amused by, and how they eat by candlelight, stumps of candles stuck onto the wooden table.

"Who pays you?" she asks.

"The government," he says, and adds that he is the proud beneficiary of two pensions, one from the sawmill factory where he was night watchman for years and the other from the state. She feels his eyes looking through her, past her, into the hall, sniffing. Can he sniff tobacco? Can he sniff the presence of a man?

"Do you still have that collection of antiquarian books?" he asks.

"They're still here," she says.

"I was telling the newcomers about them and the husband

would love to come over and have a browse . . . Fancies himself a literati."

"Once the weather picks up," she says, and arches her coat collar up around her throat, adding that she will have them over to tea later on.

"I wouldn't say no to a cup now," he says, and dilates on the fact that his sister read in a diet book that eating and drinking must be kept strictly apart and he is never given a cup of tea after his dinner of late.

"Oh, Martin," she says weakly, wearily, then asks to be excused.

"I was always welcome when the boss was here," he says, and pulls the cap down over his face, lamenting the old days when friends were friends and not acquaintances.

"*Tempus fugit*," she says, not knowing why she says it, pushing the door to shut him out.

The talk is of "your man" on the run, no scruples whatsoever, a psychopath who boasted that he would not be taken alive. It is he, her guest. Who else can it be? She has to stop herself from asking for a description of this man, this psychopath, from asking about his hair, his height, his accent, and so forth. Twenty murders, if not more, to his name. Wanted on all sides, his own side and the other side. A bit of a soloist in his deeds. Would stop at nothing. In gaol had a scheme to have two hundred pounds of explosives brought in, in a digger. Was prepared to have the whole place blown up, staff wardens, et al., was only foiled because the plan which he had the gall to put inside a crucifix he'd carved was discovered. She hears too of his journey, his journey from North to South, and thence to her, how for part of it he held a girl, in a fast-food van, at gunpoint, made her drive him fifty miles, then put tape over her mouth and left her in the middle of nowhere handcuffed, with four flat tyres, had the gall to tell her that it wasn't personal.

"They'll get him, of course," he says.

"How? How?"

"House by house . . . Ditch by ditch . . . Byre by byre . . . Floorboard by floorboard."

"Oh my God." The words fall out of their own accord.

"Pisspot by pisspot," he says, glorying in the detail of it. She looks away and sees that stray dog pass again outside the window and thinks, There must be a litter of dead baby rabbits or hares for him to keep returning like that.

Evil men. Evil men. Patrick Pearse, Michael Collins, and Co., would have their brains sprayed on a roadside.

"We don't know . . . do we?"

"Of course we know . . . They are our heroes, our martyrs . . . These are men that tie a girl up or kill her and say, 'Nothing personal.' Personal, my arse."

"Oh, Martin," she says, using his full name, rather than his nickname, Marty, and wishing him gone. She had not wanted him in. Minutes after he'd gone, he had returned to tell her that he had some bad news. The very words made her quiver. The tree with her husband's initials was rotting and would brain someone ere long. How did he know it was rotting? He had studied it before pounding the knocker and wakening her from her afternoon slumber, for which he was most heartily sorry. Oh yes, he had gone across to look at the tree for sentiment's sake, to see her husband's and his brother's initials, the M the J, and the O'M as clear as if they were carved yesterday.

"Great men . . . great men," he said, and raised his teacup as if it were a chalice. It caused him to boast of their friendship: their excursions on the lake, the traps they laid for fish, the waterfowl they caught, the winter they skated, on and on.

"How do you know it's rotten?"

"Wheezing . . . wheezing like an old woman."

She has never liked him. A snooper, always snooping, always in the spot where he should not be. Was the one to break it to her, came with a Guard the night of her husband's accident.

"I'll tell you what . . . I'll bring down a chain saw and do it of a morning . . . We'll share the wood."

"I'll have to think about it."

"Christ, you're all uptight," he says. He has noticed her fingers opening and shutting, the nails gnawed.

"It's a touch of flu."

"Oh, it's going . . . it's doing the rounds . . . It seems it's a Siberian flu."

"Yes, I'd be better off in bed," she says, half rising to give him a hint.

"You want to be careful in that bed, that some lunatic doesn't come bursting through your door with a weapon, threatening to blow your brains out."

"I lock my doors and my windows."

"That's nothing to them . . . A bit of tape around a window, a diamond to cut it, and they're in like panthers . . . There was a man in Dublin, in bed with his wife, watching TV, when a guy burst through the door with a machine gun, calls the wife a lying cunt, and tells the man to get up and get dressed . . . they're going walkies."

"Yes, that was terrible," she says weakly.

"Do you remember the man's ordeal . . . The little matter of his fingers . . . three of them amputated . . . for starters."

"Don't, Martin. Don't go over it," she says, and put her hands to her mouth as if she might retch.

"I'm telling you . . . Got a chopping board, plonked it on the unfortunate man's hand, got chisel and hammer, set to, and slowly relieved him of his finger joints; put them in Kleenex and sent one of his gang to the chapel with the ransom note."

"Terrible . . . terrible," she says, meaning to stop him, but he continues unabated.

"They were to be left under the thirteenth Station of the Cross, but would you believe it, the thug, the second in command, didn't know one Station of the Cross from another, so the bleeding fingers lie there in vain. Result. More threats . . . More agro . . . The psychopath is worried about the bad publicity and goes into a bar and orders a mineral and then comes out of the bar and fires into the car park where his girlfriend is fleeing . . ."

"The man escaped in the end, didn't he?"

"Escaped, in the end! Imagine the poor man having to hold up his bandaged fingers for twenty-three days, be moved from one house to another, stuffed under a stairs or in a hall, in the gorse and once, lying next to his bodyguard, hearing a search party of Guards out looking for him and not being able to do a damn thing."

"I can imagine it."

"I hope you can, for your own sake and for the country's sake. When they capture the hobo he goes all yellow, passes out, says, 'I'm fading . . . I'm fading fast.' Nothing about the policeman, with enough lead pumped into his stomach to galvanise a corpse . . . Nothing about him and his family," he says, and launches into a magnificat about the heroic work the Guards do, the risks they take, so that people like him and her can sleep sound in their beds.

"Talk of the word," she says, and apologises for wanting to be in her bed.

"You look shook," he says, does not move, and slugs the cold dregs of tea with intent.

"I'm afraid you'll have to leave, Martin," she says, rising, and then grips the back of the chair because of being overcome by dizziness. He takes his time, puts his arms into the sleeves of his coat, buttons it, then unbuttons it as if absentmindedly, all the while staring towards the window as if there is someone outside staring back in. The crows congregating and croaking cease their chatter for an instant, stilled, as if in answer to a warning from beyond.

"The calm before the storm," he says, and rises. What can he mean? Perhaps he means the crows coming in at dark and, just prior to settling down, doing cartwheels in the sky, moving in a beautiful fugue, as if suspended on the lower skin of the sky. To him it means mission completed. A woman on her own, claiming to be bedridden, taking a good five minutes to answer a door, reluctant to bring him to the kitchen, and when he does penetrate there, what does he subsequently see on the draining board but two of everything, two plates, two skin plates, two cups and saucers where they had tea or coffee.

"Wired to the moon," he says.

"Indeed they are," she says, and almost spryly now she sees him out and assures him that she shall think about the tree, but of course he must realise that there is a great sentimental value attached to it, what with the initials that have stood the ravages of time.

"Sentimental, my arse," he says. If it were not for the fact that he is working *sub rosa* for the government, sussing out these very criminals, he would snuff her, there and then, take her by the neck and hold her till there was not a drop of breath left. It's what she deserves. In Christ's name, why? If she were a younger woman maybe, but hunt her orchid and a man would find what—"*Sheela-na-gig.*"

"How do you know that I gave nothing away?" she says. They are in the hall, her back against the rungs of the stairs, where he pinioned her the moment her caller left, to ask what was said, every last word of it. No longer the calm or fellow feeling of their little tête-à-têtes in the morning room. His true self now. Hard. Rough. Nervy.

"Did you or didn't you?" he says.

"Cooped up in my room . . . Not knowing what's going to happen to me . . . What not . . . My fingers . . . My fingernails . . . Bits of me . . . When does it start . . . Where's the hammer, where's the chisel? Do you shoot long range or close range . . . Answer me, answer me. Look into my eyes . . . have the guts to do that. Maggots, that's what you are, you and your lot with homilies about justice . . . peace and dignity."

"Simmer down," he says. The maggot word has hurt, hit home.

"Simmer down!" she says, and asks if he would be so kind as to let her go to her bedroom because of her palpitations.

"Nothing's going to happen to you." He says it once, twice, three times, then brings his face close to hers and tells her in feck's name to tell him what the man said and get it over with.

"I've already told you . . . 'A calender of your atrocities,' pictures of you nightly on the television . . . Posters outside every barracks . . . Wanted . . . Wanted."

"What else?" he says.

"What else . . . He wants to bring down a chain saw to cut at a tree."

"When?"

"When I tell him I want it cut."

"You passed him a note."

"Yes, I wrote your nickname on the back of his hand . . . Hosta!" She knows that she is shrieking, knows that the containment or the so-called containment of the five days has broken down and that she has no inkling of what she will say or do next.

"Does he or does he not suspect that there's someone here?"

"I'm not a mind reader."

"Don't mess me." His face is so close to hers now that she smells the peppermint chocolate which she gave him after lunch. His flounder so hateful to her that she wants to prolong it, to bask in the stench of his disarray. Her own fear so bizarre that she feels fearless.

"Did you grass?"

"No, but I wish I had."

"Why didn't you, if you wish you had?"

"Because for five days and five nights I have been telling myself that you are a nice young man . . . and that you wouldn't kill and that you haven't killed. I've been telling myself this fairy tale."

"I told you I'd killed . . . The day you asked me which part I shot, I said the biggest part."

"So you did . . . and I thought that by being here . . . that by us talking . . . something would happen . . . A sea change. I'd save you . . . You'd see the light; you'd quit."

"That's nuts . . . Nothing will make me quit . . . ever."

"I see that now. I see the hatred bred in your eyes. He told me, my caller, that you said you will never be taken alive."

"True."

"I hope they take you alive, not out of mercy, but so that you'll live and relive every second of every crime."

"You're the first Irish person that's talked to me like that."

"They're too afraid to talk to you . . . You've silenced them all . . . silenced us all."

Thinking that perhaps he's going to put a hand on her, he's going to strike her, to rout this hysteria, she breaks loose and goes to his quarters, where she has not dared go before.

It takes her a moment to adjust to the semi-darkness. Black stuff drapes the window and is secured down at the four corners with brass tacks. It was the lining for a coat that never got made. Two rifles lie side by side on the bed, like two suits of clothing. Next to his bed on a chair there is a torch, a radio no bigger than a matchbox, and a photograph of a woman. She cannot make out the features, but the woman has short curly hair and is pensive.

"Your babies," she says, going across to where the guns are and lifting one, careless as to whether or not it is loaded.

"For feck's sake," he says.

"You haven't got the courage to kill me, have you . . . To look into my grey eyes and say, 'Smile . . . smile while I shoot.' " The five days have unhinged her and she knows it.

"I didn't come here to kill you."

"But you've come to kill someone."

"I haven't said so."

"No, you haven't said so, but you haven't come here for the lemonade."

"No, I haven't come for the lemonade . . . That's not my job."

"And you have a woman, I see . . . a sweetheart."

"Why shouldn't I have a woman?"

"Because you have no feelings . . . You are devoid."

"I have plenty of feelings."

"Oh yuh . . . To run up a hill, lay a booby trap, and see British soldiers blown to smithereens or, rather, not see them . . . Be gone to your safe house to roll a cigarette. Sometimes you even get the wrong men."

"We do . . . They call it the Paddy factor," he says, the eyes rabid now, shavings of slashed gold, a pent-upness, so much so that she believes he will explode.

"And you always have your arsenal ready," she says, touching the second gun, feeling the curve of the trigger.

"A rat got in here this morning."

"Aren't I looking at one?" she says, and goes out, fear and rage alternating in her.

"I never wanted us to talk . . . It was your idea . . . I came here because I understood you were in a home."

"I was in a home, but I came back to die in my own bed . . . And if you don't mind, I'd rather die in one piece."

"Most people would," he says coldly.

"Except maybe yourself . . . Maybe you like the carnage."

"If you think that I like killing for the sake of killing, you're nuts . . . You're like all the others."

"Sooner or later it will all blow up in your face," she says, mortified at the fact that she has ever allowed herself to fraternise with him.

"I expect you're right," he says as she goes out. She does not even reply. Something wiped out in his nature, his human nature.

It is against military rules that I do this, but something makes me do it. First of all, please forgive me if I have made you sick. I'll go straight to the matter. No one knows or cares about our struggle. They think we're cowboys or animals or worse. You think it too. I know that now after your outburst in the hall this morning and I even understand it. But for one minute look at it from my side of the street. Don't worry, I am not going to give you a 1916 litany. Not to grow up in hate, not to have been Papist leper scum, not to have been interned at fourteen and fifteen and sixteen, not to have been in the Crum and Longkesh and waiting to go on the blocks, now that would have been out of this world. To be an ordinary bloke with a wife and kids—I just can't imagine it. Not to have screws and RUCs tell you they'll get your sister or your mother or your aunt, that would be a bonus. Fuck them, I couldn't care less. What I would love is for you to have met some of the boys that I was in the blocks with and on the blanket with, lads of eighteen and nineteen, the bravery they showed, the craic they made; it only takes being with people like that and one's faith is invincible. I have one wish—I am afraid I don't pray—that all the deaths have not been in vain.

Mo Chara Sláin Go Fóill.

Mac

"My friend, health forever." The handwriting was minute, each letter a tilting capital. It was in black ink and folded again and again, the way he must have learned in jail, so as to be able to send requests out. He had left it on the bottom step of her bit of stairs, propped against a cup, where she must see it. She had not come out of her room since her outburst, had simply sat in her chair willing her stamina and her balance to come back. She had not felt hungry or thirsty. There had been no stirrings from him either, the house quiet as if sacked, creaks at odd moments, dry tetchy creaks. She found it when she went down towards dark and carried it up to read it. For some reason she is shaking. She cannot say why she is shaking, but she is.

Afterwards she did not feel hungry. It lay under the lamp, the black capitals so small, so helpless.

She could not say his name, so she simply said, "You . . . you . . ."

He walked faster than she had ever seen any man walk, so fast that he seemed not like a man but a wraith, and yet it was he. He had left—bag and baggage, guns and all. She had gone down to discuss the contents of his letter and found the room so emptied, so devoid of his traces that it resembled those sickrooms of her childhood, when after a death, particularly from tuberculosis, the rooms were scoured and disinfected with lime.

"Come back here." The sound of her voice was muffled in

fog, and after some time it became as if she had no voice at all. It fails her as her feet are failing her in the oversized Wellingtons, the only ones to hand in the hall, and her husband's overcoat, in the pocket of which she had found a shrivelled chestnut.

On impulse she decided to follow him as she heard him go out. He was heading for the lake, a boat maybe, to spirit him away. The words he had used—Justice . . . Identity . . . Community. What did these words mean? What value had they against the horrors of a crime? The frenzy of the pursuit does not occur to her yet. All she wants is to catch up with him.

She slips, stumbles, searches for a gap that leads to the next field, but bested by fog she cannot find it and each time crashes into a frieze of hawthorn or blackthorn that scrapes her face. As for shouting, she has given it up.

"There should be a gap here, or here," she says, weaving back and forth in search of it, the mist thick and impenetrable, a timeless, placeless, featureless world that could be the beginning or the end of creation. Her hands will have to act as compasses, first one hand and then the other, except that they are still and cold as a frozen pea packet.

"I can't go back and I can't go forward," she says, and thinks that something will come, some gatepost or landmark will tell her where she is and be a guide as to what to do, except that it doesn't, and the thistles that she grasps as props feel black and wet like slime. She talks to herself, to give herself courage—

"*Can you feel the ground*

Can you feel your feet inside the Wellingtons

Can you say hello" and hearing it said aloud, it seems so wan and ridiculous, as ridiculous as the journey she had set out on an hour or so before.

After an age it seems to her that this walking is useless. He has gone, disappeared into thin air, and what she must do is make her way back home, except that she cannot find the path. The fog has got into her mind. What she wanted really. To blot out those five days and his presence and what he stood for. To get home and lie down and call life normal again, except that her blood is freezing and her feet fail her as she weaves back and forth, and later her mind starts to go. The fog and damp are inside her brain. In the end, yelling, unhinged, she staggers from side to side, then stumbles and falls and thinks, It is not a bad thing, it is a good thing, it is only till daylight comes, and I will be on my way again . . . And . . . And.

"Lovely soft rain . . . The ground could do with it." A head of brown hair over an ironing board. Where is she? Where am I? she asks. A small room crammed with things, a low window uncurtained, and the bed on which she is sleeping only inches from the floor. There are geraniums on the windowsill, stalks high and knotty, the rust-coloured husks a shell of pink where the blossom had lain.

"Where am I?" Josie asks, and asks again, baffled.

"You're here."

"Where is here?"

"Here is here," the young voice says.

"I don't know you," she says, looking across at a beautiful young girl with a round eager face and a crop of brown hair with glints in it.

"You're in my room."

"How did I get here?"

"How did you get here . . . How d'you think!"

Josie looks about and sees nothing she recognises. There are clothes in boxes and on hangers at the back of the door, there's a poster of a film star smoking a cigarette, and on the chair beside her a big brass sulky clock. Reaching out she feels her side combs on the floor, those and a pitcher of water which she almost overturns.

"He brought you here . . . carried you," the girl tells her, and gradually and confusedly she remembers the walk at night, the fog, going round and round, trying to get to the lake, falling down and trying but not able to get up again, her legs frozen stiff like logs, and someone—she could not tell who—picking her up and shaking her, and then a boat journey, and all of her a-wander, her brain at last letting go, letting go of thought and letting the fog in.

"He found you out in the fields . . . raving. He brought you in the boat and then up from the shore and he put you into my mother's arms."

"I remember none of that . . . I was out . . . out of my mind."

"He said, 'She has a fever, look after her.' "

"I'm sorry for being such a nuisance."

"You could have died."

"I could have died," she says, and smiles wanly. She is in a flannel nightgown in a strange room and smells a geranium in the room and a dinner smell from somewhere beyond.

"What time is it?"

"It's nearly dinnertime," the girl says, and warns that she'll have to eat a bit or she'll fade away.

"What day is it?"

"Tuesday."

"What's your name?"

"I'm Creena . . . I was Margaret, but I'm Creena now. I prefer it."

"And where is . . ." She is unable to say his name, since she has never said it.

"Gone . . . In a hole somewhere. He brought you here and left . . . The Guards were after him . . . They came here, but you were too sick to talk. We did the talking."

"Who's we?"

"My mother and me . . . They know my mother. My father was in prison for fifteen years. My mother gives them hell . . . She says, 'Oh, here come the Black and Tans.' They wanted to know how we knew you and how we found you, and my mother said we knew you for years and her brother out setting traps for eel found you at the lake, wandering . . . That bit was true, you were talking raimeas."

"Saying what?"

"You said, 'Come to the fort . . . come to the fort at Kylegranagh . . .' You said, 'To cut the ropes, we're tying you to the saddle . . . Come to the fort.' "

"Strange . . . strange . . . Something in a schoolbook, I think."

"My mother knew what to do . . . She put poultices of hot meal on you, and you sweated and sweated and sweated. You wanted to go out . . . You asked to go home to your mother and father . . . Said their names . . . Bridget and Michael . . ."

"It's all a blur."

"The Guards went to your house that night. He wasn't there . . . You wasn't there . . . There was nothing . . . They rifled it . . . God knows what it looks like. A bit like my room," she says, and laughs.

"Who's that?" Josie says, pointing to a picture of the young man with a face like a lance and a wide spumy smile that was also a laugh, drenched in spume.

"You don't know who that is?"

"No."

"Shame on you. That's James Dean . . . That's Jimmy Dean."

"Is he your hero?"

"Not really." And here she looks down not at the mound of ironing but at her feet, as if to hide their size. She's wearing black stockings and stout black shoes, and yet there is a litheness to her, as if she might just float.

"And you gave up your bed," Josie says.

"My mother and me would do anything for McGreevy. She knew you too . . . She knew that your husband died up the mountains . . . Her own husband died after he came out of jail . . . Died of asthma. But the Guards still pester us . . . They come looking for things. They open drawers and look for letters and papers, send them skyways . . . They'll find nothing here, only Jimmy Dean."

Some garments she studies, then takes against and tosses them either back into the basket or onto the floor. Others she irons with a diligence, taking pride in it, bending over the ironing board and sniffing the warm cloth. Holding a denim shirt up to her chest, she compares its size with her own girth and starts to fold it, slowly, slowly, feeling the sleeves in lieu of the arms inside them.

"He comes back for clothes," she says in answer to a question not asked and describes him coming in drenched, muck on his boots, but never a moan or a mention of where he's been.

"You like him?"

"Sshh . . . I don't want anyone to know. I don't want my mother to know . . . She likes him herself, but that's different. You couldn't not . . . What I'm thinking is that the fightin' will be over in a few years . . . The South will go up there and reclaim the six counties and life will be normal and he'll come to me." And here she thinks and holds the shirt and recalls his coming in a window late one night, giving her the fright of her life, having to hold her, to comfort her, and saying, "You're a lovely girl, Creena."

She puts the things she has ironed on the bed, kicks the basket full of clothing to one side, and cannot, no matter how hard she tries, succeed in folding up the ironing board. She tries one way, then another, then goes back to the first, and still it bests her, so that eventually she slings it under the bed and scolds it.

"You're a lovely girl, Creena. That's how it begins, isn't it . . . That's how it happens. Someone coming in a window at night."

It's not, Josie thinks to say, but does not say it. Why take the plumpness out of the arms, why quench the gaud of blue in the eyes, why hasten the winter chilliness that will come anyhow?

Suddenly Creena is handing her something—it is a handkerchief sachet, faintly perfumed, and, inside, a ruled page folded tight. Soon as she hands it, she is gone.

Into the riven
Breast
Of a proud
Heart
A pauper's fate
Was cut.
You resolved
In the terrible
Moon
And the drip
Of night
To do
What you must do.
You keep it to yourself.
You cannot know

How your life
Reaches
Into mine.

Through the jamb of the door she watches, half a smile on her face, then suddenly flinches and rushes in to grab it, believing that she has done something wrong.

"Old people know nothing about young love," she says, scrunching it up.

"That's not . . ." The thin bony hand going up to interject and the voice so different now, soaked in the yeast of memory.

A Love Affair

Summer evening, the gnats and pismires suspended in the air, the dandelions scaldingly bright, and an urgency in her limbs, a precognition of what was to be. Why him? Why that man and not another? It was his eyes she first responded to, a sort of indigo colour, with thick black brows which had the odd silver hair and gave them a look of marcasite; fevered eyes which, for all their modesty, had had some compact with the devil. He was down by the lake casting a line, and when he saw her he dropped his rod, allowing it to bow and wobble of its own accord, a mimicry of what would happen if a fish had been taken. She'd gone out to look for a hen that strayed, did it every year at the same time, hatching time, decided to lay her eggs and to hatch her young out-of-doors, a wild biddy she was.

"Oh, Father," she said. He was a new priest and had said only two Masses and had delivered no sermons. Looking at the fishing net, brown and scraggly, she said somewhat archly that it seemed he had not any luck at all. He had caught a perch but let it go. The previous evening he had caught an eel.

"An eel," she said, much too loud. The thin eels refusing to die, wriggling in the pan while still being cooked, always gave her the shivers, and she told him so. Did she like fishing? he asked.

"Haven't the patience," she said, and added that men seemed more suited to that pastime than women. He smiled. His smile was utter, every muscle in his face went into it. Did she like walking? Oh yes, of an evening, to pass the time. It seemed quite blasé when she said it like that; it did not seem like a woman primed to flee her own house and flee the prison of her own white body and go somewhere, anywhere, escape. When she thought of her body she thought of those large dead fish which she had seen in a fish shop in Brooklyn, smothered in crushed ice, the mottled scales a-glitter. Of late she had been having some fainting fits, the staggers, as an old woman called them; people said it was blood pressure and she let them think so and dutifully got the tablets that the doctor prescribed, but crushed them between her fingers at once and spitefully put them in the hens' food. Good for the hens' blood pressure. Yes, she liked to walk, especially in the spring, bluebells, hawthorn blossoms, things like that.

His eyes were dark, the same dark as the ink at school, but she reckoned that it could be the light, the evening light, and for all she knew, her own eyes were dark too and swimming with a sort of exuberance. His eyes and his gabardine coat were almost the same colour and his skin was sallow. A shadow. A man who might come from behind a tree, embrace a person, and disappear again. He told her that he had once taken a walking holiday in the Alps in the spring and that the wildflowers, especially the gentians, were among the most exquisite that he had ever seen.

"In the snow . . ."

"In the thaw . . . Water everywhere . . . The sound of running water and the flowers."

"When was that?"

"Oh, that was . . . before I was ordained," and by the way

he said it, she felt that there had been some doubt in his mind about being ordained and that perhaps he had gone there or had been sent there to wrestle with his conscience.

"I was looking for a hen," she said, and proceeded to walk off, tapping a bit of stick, a hazel that she had picked up on her way, hoping that he was not looking after her, observing her awkwardness. Hatching time. A hen quite satisfied to sit on her eggs for the bulk of the day, getting up only to gobble at a bit of mash. Was she like that? Hatching time. Spring. Thaw. The wildest impulses that befell one, the almost irrepressible longing to run back and grasp his arm and convey something—gentian stars wrung from a wintery cusp.

Things begin so nonchalantly, especially clandestine things. A burnished welcome, every single feature in the big room lit up, the fire flames dancing on this and that so that the mirrors shone like billy-o, and on the silver salver could be seen a heated underlay of copper over which silverplate had been thinly sprayed. The cranberry glasses looked bewitching, like those jars in the apothecary window in Wine Tavern Street which she had seen on her honeymoon. This too a honeymoon of sorts. Father John had been invited and was in their sitting room, in their midst, the very same as a bank clerk or one of the dappers, and their not having to call him Father at all, this at his request. He had been to Holland since he had seen them, at a conference discussing with other priests how to modernise Mother Church. He was describing the landscape—unending low land, the cumulus skies, downpours of rain, water mills, their red roofs the colour of cocks' combs.

"Cocks' combs," she shrieked, surprised at the word. She must soften her voice, modulate it, or her husband would wonder.

"Rain you say?" James said.

"Buckets of it," he said.

"Like ourselves," James said.

"Ah, but no mountains," the priest said, and gave a kind of valedictory salute with his hands to the beauty of the mountains beyond the long windowpanes, then going so far as to postulate that mountains lend weight to the national character.

"In what way?" she ventured to ask.

"Variety, complexity, momentum," he said.

"Variety, complexity, momentum," she repeated. The drawing room had never heard such words and the silverware and pewter responded to them, and in the grate a swag of orange gold fluttered merrily up the chimney. Variety, complexity, momentum.

He had also seen some great paintings, interiors and exteriors, and had stood in front of *The Nightwatch* speechless that one hand could have executed a work so vast, so meditative. She could see her husband getting restless by the way he lit the next cigarette on the butt of the unfinished one, and therefore she intervened, seeing herself now as the practised hostess.

"Aren't there diamonds in Amsterdam?" she said, to which her husband countered with a recitation:

I see diamonds in Amsterdam
I see diamonds not worth a damn.

Father John smiled and said, "How true, how true," and was happy to tell them of the selection he had seen in a factory: diamonds uncut, bluish pink or smoky black in their raw state, others made into jewels after they had been treated on a revolving cast-iron disk.

"A dop," he told them it was called.

"Fancy that," she said. One of her cheeks blazed, but the

other side was flushed too, and she kept wanting to kick her legs, to kick high up, to the oak beams, and show her underthighs, sheer in a pair of mauve silk stockings that had been part of her trousseau. She had felt this restlessness once before, with a married man, a Jewish man in Brooklyn, a dinner guest in the house where she worked who had followed her into the kitchen to give her a tip, gave her a silver dollar, and, rather than handing it, had slipped it into her bosom with a "Keep it warm." She had allowed the hand to lift one breast and hold it as if it were a cloth purse. She had taken an illicit walk with that selfsame gentleman a few nights later, and passing a house of ill fame, he had stopped and said to her, "How would you like it if I took you in there for an hour or two?" and though much too constrained to reply, she had in part yielded, a loosening, as if she was already inside, on a couch being undressed, or on a low bed being ravaged by him, oblivious to the seediness on all sides, a grotto for him.

She returned from her reverie to find the two men laughing, boisterous laughing such as is heard only when a good joke is cracked.

"Did you hear that?" Jamie was saying.

"I was miles away," she said with a certain hauteur.

"Father John saw rough diamonds," her husband said, and laughed again, all of him laughing, his eyes laughing with a riotous mirth.

"Rough diamonds?" she said, and looked at Father John, who though his laughter was more refined was relishing the joke all the same.

"Scutty little things," Jamie said, adding that they were like bits of pebble, nothing more.

How had she missed it, how long had her thoughts and her juices wandered to the house of ill fame with steps up to it, a lantern outside the door, and pink curtains on all the windows upstairs and downstairs, the upstairs ones drawn at all times? She had gone back there, gone back alone, and stood outside.

"Rough diamonds," Jamie repeated, and wondered where in God's name the supper was, for weren't these two rough diamonds, Father John and himself, ravenous?

In the kitchen she bustled. Everything was ready, the slices of roast duck and orange sauce in the lower oven, potatoes in their jackets piping hot, the skins falling away nicely, and the turnips mashed to a T and flavoured with pepper, salt, and nutmeg. The apple pie was still baking, in a pot oven with coals on top and coals underneath, some of which had petered out. As she bent to get a few hot coals from the fire, she felt a presence. She knew by the shiver that passed through her that it was not her husband, that it was he. Like zigzags of cold run amok inside heat. He had come to help himself to another glass of lemonade, claiming that he had never tasted anything so delicious, that it knocked spots off the bottled stuff, adding that she should patent it.

"I'm honoured," she said.

Holding the tongs towards him, the red coals between the buckled levers looking decidedly dangerous, she posed a riddle.

Long legs, crooked thighs,
Small head and no eyes—riddle?

"A tongs," he said, and smiled, giving her one of the softest, most meaningful lover looks that she had ever had. He touched her then. They touched without touching, each remaining motionless but transfixed, the glide already commenced.

"Do those gongs work?" he asked, pointing to the ten green verdigreed gongs ranged above the dresser.

"They do . . . They'd make your blood race."

"Then ring them," he said, and went out with an air of

defiance, and presently the brassy, bongy sounds, so penetrant, so audacious, resonated through the house.

To shower him with things, worldly things, and the fruits of nature. Looking at the thrushes so sleek and plump, she longed to catch them with her bare hands and grill them and serve them on toast for him, the way they did in southern Italy. It was he who told her so. He also told her of Samson becoming entangled in the long tresses of Delilah's hair. He told her myriad things, a story he had read once called "Raspberry Water" by a Russian, a story about hunting folk. Sometimes he was silent. He just looked at her; she could feel his eyes following cravenly as she went about doing her work.

Out there in the kitchen garden she gathered branches and blossoms, tore at the rhododendron leaves and picked the few flowers that were in bloom. He came faithfully each morning and stayed all day, lolling in the chair, accepting whatever she offered him, and remarking on little touches to her appearance or the kitchen itself.

Hurrying in, she laid the green branches on the table, and the sight of them was like a scene pictured in the Gospels or a Bible she once had. She should get ointments with which to anoint him. Yes, things were becoming headier.

The few flowers in the big jug looked scant, so she put them instead in a tureen, where they drifted like water lilies, their cheeks touching. They had rose-pink cheeks and were ruffled at the edges.

"What is that flower?" he asked, examining the face of one and the glossy backdrop of leaf.

"A camellia," she said. She had been sent it as a gift; it had come in the post, a low bush in its clay bedding, wrapped in sacking and the name printed on a tag—Debutante. One of the dapping gentlemen had sent it. It did not like the soil, or else the frost got it, because no more than two or three blooms appeared each year, and now she had picked them and put them sailing in water for him to admire. The apple blossoms were everywhere, on the table, on the chairs, and in spatters on the flagged floor.

Soon as he saw her pick up the yellowed book, his hands went up in defence to signify no. She teased him and asked if it was against his religion. It was a very old book which she had found in a trunk and which she often consulted. Different symbols, painted in black, signified a different set of destinies. By asking a certain question and then, blindfolded, putting one's finger on one of the symbols, one knew which answer to consult. He did not want to know his future, he was quite happy with the present.

"And what's this?" he said, pointing to her bitten nails. Why had she taken to biting her nails? She pulled her hands back and denied it, said they broke off, something lacking in her diet.

"You're not happy," he said.

"It can get gloomy," she said, and looked about somewhat flustered and moved the dish of flowers to another part of the table.

"To whom do you go for comfort?"

"Nobody . . . My religion," she said, and wondered if he saw that she was lying, because in fact her religion had never been a comfort, never throughout the early years of her marriage, when she looked out at the listless fields, at the teacloths and underclothes flapping on the clothesline, the mutinous bullocks mounting each other in sport or desperation, and swore at the tassle of the window blind that for no noticeable reason went rat-a-tat-tat . . . rat-a-tat-tat at given times.

"Your religion," he said, but without sounding convinced. She asked him if he had ever had a crisis of religion himself. He thought for a moment. Then he looked at her, one of those soft nighttime looks that made her melt, and he steeled himself and said, "I'm not going to answer that." She saw by the terror in his expression that he was smitten with her and doing everything to stamp it out, but that each morning when he visited, it was reignited, like a gorse bush that has seemingly quenched but that needs only a puff of wind to be set ablaze again.

"Bitter aloes . . . That is the thing, to put on your nails, to check your nasty habit," he said. She did not like the word nasty. He found an old newspaper behind the cushion of his chair and began to read it as if engrossed.

"Men are all moods," she said, busying and humming, incorrigible in her prism of happiness.

"What is it at all?" Jamie said, balancing it on his palm so that he could inspect it thoroughly. Two pale concave disks of wood, saucer-shaped, wedged against each other at a peculiar angle. The wood was very white, as if pickled in brine or snow. Father John had brought it back from one of his travels, where he had been at an Ecumenical Council.

"Your guess is as good as mine," she said, and tried to hide her pleasure at her first gift from him.

"Does it have a name?"

"I think he said *Cloudberries*," she said.

"*Cloudberries*," he said, tilting the one disk that could be moved slightly, and then he became very animated and said should they not christen it, give it a name, a boy's name or a girl's name. He knew his wife well, as well as anyone knew her, and beneath the folds of her petticoat he knew something gamey had begun.

"Christen it!" she repeated, the word too meaningful, too dangerous.

"If you'd had a boy, you'd have called him John or James,

and a girl, you probably would have called her Mary or Kate or both," he declared.

"I'd call her Eleanora," she said defensively, but not glancing up at him. What did he read in her—a late heat, like those marigolds or roses that flower a second time or birds with two broods of young.

"I'll tell you what . . . we'll call it *The Snowy-breasted Pearl,*" he said, and suddenly he began to sing. Through the hushed and overbright air, the words were being aimed at her, the voice admitting to its several ranges, tenor then bass, his hands thumping the table at times and holding down the long sad chords and the sad words to emphasise their plight:

If to France or far-off Spain
She'd crossed the watery main
To see her face again
The sea I'd brave.
And if 'tis heaven's decree
That mine she may not be
May the Son of Mary me in mercy save.

She saw tears starting up in his eyes and thought, He knows, he knows. If she could have held him then. But she could not hold him. Her only thought was, He has given me a gift, Father John has given me a gift, and the thought grew bigger and sturdier each time she said it, like a child swelling up in her.

"Tell you what . . . Stuff it in with your undies," he said, handing it to her roughly, and the look in his eyes was not plaintive but vehement and purposeful.

As he reached in for the tin of bicarbonate she knew that he was about to mix himself a dose for his bile, but that before evening he would have headed for the village and be on the batter before night.

O thou blooming milk-white dove
To whom I've given true love
Do not ever thus reprove my constancy.

She half sang it, half spoke it, following him to the back kitchen, where he had gone to get spring water from the bucket.

"You've no air . . . You're tone-deaf," he said.

"You're the singer in this family."

"And what are you?" he asked, stirring and restirring the fizzy medicine, then drinking it in one long, disgusted gulp.

Insects prey on her and she swats them with a switch of dock leaf. The spot she has chosen is cool, slightly damp, a knoll under a tree, and she is glad of it because of her body perspiring so, despite having put cologne on.

She will have cooled off by the time he has come and everything will be cooler and moister from the oncoming night. She is early. Deliberately so. She needs to be lying down when he gets there, in case her knees or her stance give her away. It's a distance up from the lake, yet she can hear the old boatman hammering away, the harsh clanging of the metal not at all jarring but a comfort because of being so steady and ongoing. It is this they will hear. Probably they will not say much. She feels that he will appear suddenly and lie next to her and in a silence they will couple, their shadow selves going beyond the gates of propriety to the deeper hungers within. A rose he said she was. Many-folded, folds he would open back, pleat after pleat of rose-hued flesh.

"Darn it," she says of the new corset that pinches and ridges her stomach. Being new, the hooks are slow to separate, so that she must start with a bottom one, then the top one, and gradually ease them away. Flung there, the pink broderie anglaise looks like a cloth spread out for a picnic, in the dusk.

She flings it a distance away. Darn it. What would he smell of? Tobacco. How she loved the particular little black cigarettes that he smoked, a brand he discovered on his travels in Holland, a cross between a cigarette and a cigar. They were thin and sinewy, and often after he had left her house she put the gold-tipped butts to her lips and let her tongue circle them.

She listens for a footstep, knowing that he will have parked his car a distance away. She does not think beyond his coming, his lying next to her, the nearness of their bones; she does not think beyond it to the night, to going home, to some excuse or other, her husband watching her at the opposite end of the kitchen, her secret blurred in the fidgety light of the tilly lamp, because by then she will be different, more contained.

The dark gives her courage to undo the bun at the back of her hair and allow the mass of hair to fall forward, to speak through it, mouthing the secret and heartfelt words that she has rehearsed. The first moments will tell everything, will tell for instance if they are mismatched; but why ask such a thing when she knows they are meant, like tubers under winter bedding, and how it was evident the moment when he described the thaw in the Swiss mountains, the water gushing in and out between rills and valleys, the flowers, the violet excrescences being born out of the seams of rock, like floats of jewellery, the faces soft, silken, the underneath parts swished and swaddled in damp.

As time goes on, she picks the pine needles out of her hair and takes to counting them, to making predictions with them, but not once does she lose heart, because she knows that his need to possess her is, if anything, more scalding than her own. She pictures his car, the Peugeot, backing out from the chapel grounds, the spill of his hair for a moment obscuring his vision, him irked because some parishioner has detained him, and she pictures the eyes shy and miscreant and his reaching out to her with his boyish plea to slap him for being late.

Sounds carry more: cars, a donkey braying, the myriad wheezes of cattle, the boatman silent, and she imagines foxes and badgers coming out of their holes with their stares and their all-day hunger to be satisfied. The sight of a moon—large, lopsided, and very orange—tells her that it is getting late.

"It is not the end, it is merely a setback." This now her Rosary, her recitation.

She walks listlessly through the pine grove into the fields past cattle and stone cairns, the smell of cattle dung and cattle flesh, and in the humid air the cloying smell of elderflower, and she thinks this field will always carry the essence of him. Not rose memory now but ugly things, lumpen, brutish, that awful depletingness, like a big goose egg being skewered with a knitting needle, the juices leaking and dripping out of her and falling onto the toughened after-grass.

"Take that, and that . . . and that"—the sound of the smacking almost pleasant, mimicking the smacking of the butter patter itself on the soft curds of half-formed butter, but the blows vicious and scalding as they land on her flesh. The patter was the first thing that came to his hand as he leapt at her from the kitchen. She was grasping the ladder, her eyes closed, allowing no whimper of pain or even protest to escape her lips. He was too mad for that. A cuckold. A cuckold. He said the word with venom. Where had he learned it? Paud—the unwitting cause of this atrocity—out foddering cattle had come on the corset and, thinking that it had blown off the clothesline, had brought it back as a trophy, proud of his diligence. He had given it to James, who might not have thought anything suspicious but for the note tucked in at the top of the spiral. Earlier she had written their two names to play the love-like-hate-adore-marry game, a device simply arrived at by crossing out the corresponding letters on both names, and she had come up with the fact that Father John adored her and that she would marry him. She had used her maiden name. It told everything. First, and with gusto, Jamie marched towards her with the outheld corset asking, "Have you seen this, missus?" duping her into the ready-made lie of saying that it must have blown off the hedge, as things often did.

"Shit and shite," he said then, thrusting the note to her mouth like a bandage.

"And this," he said. Her handwriting quivered before her, as did the sad farce of their pretending that Father John was a family friend. Threats, shouts, expletives as he chased her down the hall, up one flight of stairs and then another, while she made for the bedroom, remembering how that morning Paud had cleaned the windows and hoping the ladder might still be there. She saw herself slam the bedroom door and pull the bolt, which she knew would yield to the slightest pressure, as she made a dash to the raised window to escape. She had almost succeeded when he burst in, caught her beam, and with a savage alacrity slammed the window down so that she was half in and half out, the wooden sash wedged into her flesh.

A fierce flagellant lather of joy possessed him on account of the pain that he could feel issuing back from her, his energy prodigal as he beat her for every drink she had ever grudged him; for his poor brother, whom she had dispatched to an exile's death; for the offspring which she had not given him; the mares and fillies she had reviled; but most of all for the dried-up menagerie of her womanhood, the farce that was their bedchamber life. She must describe it, her down-by-the-sally-garden tryst, reveal if the reverend had it in him, if he knew the ropes or had to be steered into her with his short horn. Zanily, he beat her for the pleasures he had not given her and which he believed were wantonly gratified in the woods. Nothing would make him understand that she had gone there to no avail and nothing would make her tell it. Silence was her staple now and she supped on it like a child sucking a lozenge. Hot, burning, quivering blows, and then a dampness as if maybe she had started to bleed, and her eyes damp also, but the tears being driven back in, in. It got quieter then, more methodic, strophe and anti-strophe, so that she was able to count them and almost guess when he would tire of it. Then a few last long neutral blows in which she believed she felt somewhere in him a surrender, as though he had reached a breaking point in his outrage.

The quiet was so strange after he left, after she saw him wheel his bicycle and close the gate with a vexed clang.

Time crawling by, the evening star and the Plough and other stars that she did not know the names of and cattle trudging in small groups across the shaggy field, before deciding where to settle, and the pigeons in bed with one another in the trees and the pain in her mind far surpassing the pain in her flesh. How differently the stars and the several sounds struck her compared with the night before, when she had waited for him, and she thought that not for anything would she wish him to see her naked thus, naked and cut, asprawl a windowsill.

"Good God . . . you're black and blue." The unctuous voice unable to conceal its pleasure in being lucky enough to be sent up, lucky enough to see the harm for himself and be able to memorise it for his friends in the town. It was the Snooper.

"What time is it?"

"Whatever time it is . . . The boss says you're to come down and cook a fry . . . He has company."

"He can fry his own grub."

"He won't, he's bucking."

"Lift this thing," she says, then pauses before straightening up, not knowing if she can walk and not wanting this mock sympathy—how she should do something before her wounds fester.

Down in the front room a fire going and a rough line of jaws, side by side, like men on a chapel bench, except that they are drunk, too drunk and too skittish to even look at her in her bedraggled state, and too settled to go home. She knew them, but never once, not in the pouring of the tea or serving them as she was obliged, with fried bread and sausages, did she look in their faces. There was the Snooper, an ex-postman, a knacker called J.J. who dealt in old horseflesh, brought it to the city and sold the different cuts to different dealers, the hooves being useful only for making rosaries. Egan, the auctioneer, was the only one to give some nod of gratitude when she put the plate before him. He had given her a peck once, after she had bought that chandelier. Paud refused food, looked down at his torn trousers as if he was looking at an exercise book on his knees. She could hear him breathing loudly in some sort of pointless atonement.

"Feed. Shovel. Ride. Woman and horse," James said, remarking on the likenesses in both but stressing that a horse had more honour.

"Feed. Shovel. Ride," he said, laughing, and they laughed with him to keep him amused.

"That's a good mare you have out in the front field," the knacker says.

"I have good mares in all my fields," he says, and seeing her about to depart, he drags her back and says with a galling friendliness, "Not tonight, Josephine . . . Not tonight."

By turn he was pouring whisky for them or asking them to behold her shins and carriage, then again picking on one or another, asking how such an ignorant yahoo came to be in his parlour. From time to time he enquired about her injuries, said she must be feeling a bit sore, how these blisters would have to be prodded with a safety pin, and on impulse pushed Paud in front of her and said, "Say sorry," and if that wasn't enough said, "Give her the paw"; then, as Paud started to snivel, thumping him so that he fell on her.

"An informer, nothing but an informer," Jamie said, taking him by the collar and shuffling him out.

"Tell us that story about being up in Dublin with the cattle jobber," the knacker asked, to humour him, and again she heard it, amidst grunts and splutters, how he was with a cattle jobber, how they'd had one too many, how in the digs in the North Circular Road they had to share a room with a Roscommon man, how in the morning they set out to buy cattle, not a bob between them, when lo and behold, the jobber puts his hand in his pocket and finds a wad of notes, and how instead of joy and jubilation, the eejit wondered if he'd caught some disease from the man's breeches, proceeded to strip, and in his birthday suit in the middle of the city let out roars as moronic as the animals being driven into their pens.

"What happened then?" the Snooper asks.

"What happened then . . . We did our business and we repaired to Jury's Hotel and lived like kings."

"It's a great story, Boss."

"It's a hoot."

"It's the art in the telling," the knacker says, and is asked what an ape like him would know about the art in the telling when he couldn't even sign an X on a ballot sheet.

"The art in the telling," he says, choosing not to understand the insult.

Seeing the sculpture on the whatnot next to a stuffed owl he asks that it be passed down to him.

"What do you think this thing is called?" he asks, but none of them knows. His reply is in song; he sings to it as he walks around the room with it, pawing it, then a lather of kisses.

For if not mine, dear girl,
Oh, snowy-breasted pearl,
May I never from the fair with life return.

When he stands before the fire, she knows what he is about to do. Assuring the assembled company that it will make a better smell and a better splash than either applewood or arbutus, he hurls it into the fire and waits for the flames, only to be disappointed. The two disks of wood vanish as if made of wafer, simply melt and disappear into the steeple of the soot-softened chimneypiece.

"Woman's muck," he says with a finality, warming his hands by the fire and then crossing to show his claims on her. He touches first one breast and then the other.

"You should see yourself," she says stonily.

"Rub 'em . . . Feed 'em . . . Rough 'em," he says.

"Ah now, James . . . That's going too far." It is Egan who comes forward to draw him back into the haze and revelry of the drinking.

If to France or far-off Spain
She'd crossed the watery main
To see her face again
The sea I'd brave.
And if 'tis heaven's decree
That mine she may not be
May the Son of Mary me in mercy save.

It was Egan who sang it softly and in some sort of muted apology.

Not long after, her husband stood before her, thick in tongue now, thick and slurry, eyes crinkled and crazying, not even sure if she is she or another.

"Have to see a man about a dog," he said, and staggered out.

Going queer then, mixing up flowers and birds, still things and moving things, the pods of flowers full of compressed song. From June until late September, she could be seen sitting out on the verandah of an evening gazing or talking to birds. Her husband never addressed her and, if he passed, merely made a grunt, an animal grunt. People knew about it, and knew how Paud had been sent away and knew that she was in disgrace. There was speculation as to whom it was she had had the assignation with. A foreigner, it was felt. She got anonymous letters, the same wording each time, what dirty things this person intended to do with her and what she would be compelled to do in return.

Having sat on the verandah for an hour or more, she ran up the steps of the stairs and ran down again, because just as she had wanted to be inert she suddenly wanted to be active and do something strenuous. She routed cobwebs out of their corners, fat grey things, vented her spleen on them, rapped curtains to free them of dust and association, then fled to the paddock to dig potatoes to boil for the animals. Other times she'd stand in front of the long mirror of the wardrobe and decide that the sockets of her eyes were filling up with blood. She was tasting blood. She saw her priest being boiled in oil and skinned, skinless. She talked to herself in an English accent, said, "You have not lost your looks, m'dear." The m'dear she had heard from one of the wives of the dappers, a whining woman who ruled her husband and wore a bracelet as big as a napkin ring. Often having donned a good dress she would take it off again, get into her old clothes, and run down and pump water. Bucket after bucket of it lined up in the back kitchen, just as in the season when the dappers stayed and had to have hot baths when they came in off the lake in the evenings. She'd take the buckets she had filled, two at a time, to a cow house or a hen house, swish the water all over, and sweep out the scour and the droppings, telling herself that yes, she was atoning, she was doing penance for an unlived sin. That thrush was always there. It was a weird sort of thrush, on its own, without a companion, and the sound it made was uncanny, not melodious at all. The little eyes would fix her, two treacly little eyes fix her with "M'dear." She always broke down then and went through to the flower garden to sit on the steps and retrace the sequence of things, arriving at the fateful moment when they met by the ruined cottage with the rowan trees, his eyes so pitiful, the unslept lids a mauve colour, as if faintly dyed, his saying, "You see it's not possible . . . it's not possible for me to see you or be seen with you," yet everything in the expression and the thrust contradicting what he was saying, and their reaching, reaching, past boundaries, caution thrown to the wind, his hand like a web drawing itself over hers, fingers plaiting, and his looking across to where his car was parked, the black Peugeot they'd named Herman, and his saying, "Herman and I will take you for a spin." Yes, he must recall it. He must recall her sitting in, and his giving her the bag of toffees he had brought, and their asking in jest why a toffee was a mackintosh and a mackintosh a toffee and for that matter a mackintosh also a raincoat, talking babble, their lips like fruits being squashed together, the insides raw and ravenous, that infant-like glee of two people devouring each other.

She began letters that were left unfinished. Remarks such as "I never believed it could end so" and then another time, when she lost the crown of a tooth, she remembered how he had done the same thing biting on a ring in a barm brack and she wrote, "I thought of you this morning when I bit," but didn't go on. Then when she was at her weakest she wrote, "I know that I must cross your mind from time to time. I know by the way you stood near me at the crossroads and broke my reserve." Once they were written she burnt them. She held them on the tongs and watched whilst these garbled sentiments became shreds of grey and then curls of ash, then pure nothing, effacement. She began to taste soap in her mouth. She seemed to think it was Sunlight washing soap. It touched on everything she tasted. One last meeting. She prayed for that.

Between lovers there is that something to be said, but what gets said is either too much or too little, never the one living word.

She took out the locket into which she had put a few particles of his hair from the morning when she had cut it in the kitchen. He had asked her to cut it and had brought a taper so that she could singe the scraggly bits. Taking them out she held them up to the light, black but with the merest prefiguration of grey. They would be grey in a few years' time. What would become of him? There were rumours sometimes that he was being moved and then rumours that they were just rumours. At Christmas she left a card and some hand-knitted socks, but these were never acknowledged. She had not signed the card, but she believed that he would remember their minuet with the green knitting wool, his finding her winding the skein on two chairs placed at a distance and how he had offered up his outstretched hands and they had marched throughout the house, her winding, his holding, his surprise and delight at being mischievously led into each room, and finally her bedroom, privy with him, her page, her chevalier, her groom.

A mousetrap was of that pliable pink wood, tempting as a marshmallow. It was on the counter of the hardware shop, where the owner always took an age to come out and, when he did, rebuked people, said couldn't they see he was having his tea. She took a liking to it, the wood so pink and the spring so eager that she foresaw how useful it would be. Hosts of mice used to dart across the back kitchen at night, they could hear them in the kitchen, Jamie and she, where they sat in silence. No sound at all, since they were not speaking, only the odd shuffle from the fire that passed for sound. They did not use the good rooms anymore or light fires there. Sometimes she wondered what he thought of when he looked into the flames—other women, kinder women, a less scalding destiny. She thought it too.

Once she got away with the mousetrap, she felt free to steal anything, free and audacious. She stole chocolate and pipes of licorice and fashion magazines and anything at all that was left in the chapel, odd gloves, anything. She flung them in a holdall, like trophies. It was in the drapery shop that she met her downfall. The smell of the new materials got into her and she fancied herself being elsewhere, a pampered woman being fitted for a dress, back in Brooklyn, on a box, and a woman with pins in her mouth making her turn slowly while she tacked the hem of a dance dress. The slip that she sighted had something of the same allure, turquoise with deep scallops of lace the colour of elderflowers. Soon as the young assistant went to the back to get twine she decided to do it and slipped it in its tissue into her rush bag.

"Excuse me . . . Mrs. O'Meara," the girl said, reaching to open the folds of the bag and shouting to her boss, "Can you come out quick, ma'am."

How she had pleaded with them, two women, one young, one not, both intractable; how she had said that it was her nerves, that it was the tablets she was taking, and how of course she had meant to pay for it anyhow. They were pleased to see her so craven, she who had never asked anyone to the big house, who had sat aloof at chapel and called people uncouth, at last brought low. She begged that it be carried no further and that no one be told.

"My husband will have to know of it," the shopkeeper said, triumph in her eyes.

"But I'm giving it back," she said, and held the bag upside down so that not only the slip but all the contents spewed out and rolled over the floor.

That night she told James. She had to tell him before someone else did. She put her hand out, like a supplicant, and said, "I've been found stealing," and then she stood and asked him to hold her. The way he held her was the cruelest of all. Blankness, like a blank wall, holding on to another bit of blank wall, quite slack.

"You could go to court," he said.

"I expect I could," she said. He had not even asked what it was she had stolen.

How long did it all take? How long does it take to murder first a body and then the image interred within that body, outlasting it, outliving it, refusing to give up the ghost? You know by your clothes and your shoes, your worn-out shoes that cause you to trip on a pavement. She took them to the mender's, ventured into the one-room hovel where Vinny sat alone, hammering and stitching and thonging, immune to the smell and the darkness, the smell from streets and farm-yards and cow-sheds. In one corner she sighted a pair of dance shoes, silver and purple, with a massive diamante buckle on each one, the only thing of beauty there was.

"Heels and toes, if you please," she said.

"They're finished," he said, holding one of them, then doubling it back to show her that the sole had the pliancy of cardboard or a socket.

"You'll have to get a new pair," he said.

"Do your best," she said, and threw them down among a pyramid of unsightly footwear, joined together by their laces. She was not even sure if she would ever come back for them. She thought, If he were to give me the dance shoes, if he were even to lend them to me for one night, it would give me heart. And she stood for a minute as if he might divine that thought.

Dreams in which he returned, pale, contrite, needy. Once it was his arriving on a bicycle, with three snowdrops in a pot, and his saying, "One for you . . . one for me, and one for the child." The dream was so real that she felt the clay dark and moist and palpitating, as if there were worms in it. The white flowers had a tincture of green in their centre.

Hopes, half hopes, getting fainter with time, and then one day she saw reality and it was like seeing her own name scrawled on the road, with drops of her own blood.

She took walks on Sundays to seek company, a child, a tinker, anyone. A bride who had just come to the neigh-bourhood took a liking to her and used to ask her in. In the dampish parlour that smelt of ripe and rotting apples they chatted and allowed themselves morsels from the wedding cake and bits of broken icing which were hard as chalk. The bride, being no longer young, was desperate to conceive a child and was told that it was lucky to keep some of the wedding cake for the christening, and so she did, allowing them only crumbs and then biscuits.

"Is there anything I should take . . . any tonic or herb?" she asked one Sunday.

"Nothing . . . Nothing whatsoever. It's up to God," Josie said reprovingly.

"They say there's a midwife in Galway who has herbs . . . She dopes people," the bride said then, at once fascinated and fearful of this rumour.

"How would I know about a midwife in Galway?" Josie said, standing and already realising that by her flash of temper she had gone too far, and in this she was correct, because she was not invited in again.

It was a warm Sunday, autumn, the rowan trees up at the ruined cottage a brazen blaze of red, and the summer cottages vacated, no sign of life at all, just reminders, spent fireworks and a pie dish brimming with rainwater. She decided that she would take a longer walk, maybe even go to the village to buy bread. Food meant a lot to them now. They ate more. He had moved to another bedroom, to be near the Old King Cole, as he called it. She had new shoes that hurt. The leather pressed on her big toes and her heels were skinned. Nothing for it but to sit on the ditch and wait for some passing car to hail a lift. She would wave, wave one of the new shoes if necessary. Hearing a car a little way off, she braced herself and got ready to stand up, but she was too late. It came at full speed around the corner and was his car and it was him, looking exactly as he had looked months before, boyish and with that shadowy hesitancy to him, his eyes soft until he saw her, and then a stark look and the car gathering speed and his tearing off like a man who has seen a ghost. She did not move, not yet. She sat there and thanked God that at least she had not been standing up, begging. She recalled his two expressions, the soft look and then the shock, or was it the hatred, when he saw her.

The love that she had felt for him rose up in her then and flowed through, a river wild and rapid and overwhelming, red, green, and iron-brown water swishing the lining of her body, the body that had not been allowed to nestle with him and open to him. There are moments in life when a great softness is coupled with a great hardness. Just as an instant before all had been soft and moist, there came then the spectre of the charnel house, himself, herself, like lumps of charred dough, but side by side so that she could impart her hatred of him.

"He has shown his true and callous colours . . . his true and cowardly colours," she said, mashing her feet with her hands and glad of one thing, that she had not been standing with her hand up.

"And the beautiful thing was that he never knew how much it meant to me," she said to the young girl who sat captive in the clothes basket, her legs swinging.

"And the beautiful thing was . . ." Creena repeated but could not go on.

A little frown came over her. To say such a thing would be to forgo everything, to stamp on her dreams, to crush that one dream that McGreevy would stop mourning his dead wife and come in the night and talk with her and tell her that he had come to settle. It was the only hope she had; it kept her warm, it kept her being able to milk and fodder and to go to Mass and bingo and think of the Big Dipper, not the painted one at the carnival, but theirs, his arms hoisting her up, up beyond the grey mountain to the blazing heavens.

"I'm sorry for what I said about old people and love," she said.

Eat a salt herring going to bed,
Take a cup of water to the bedside.
Future partner will come at midnight and give drink.

Josie smiles as she says it.

"Is that true?" Creena asks.

"It's supposed to be," and they laugh and wonder where they could lay their hands on a salt herring.

"What is it you love about McGreevy?"

"Everything," Creena says, and then as an afterthought: "He's a volunteer, isn't he."

Last Days

"A savage . . . Out-and-out savage."

"And a pervert to boot . . . Got the Shaughnessy youngster into a shed . . . That Imelda one."

"What happened?"

"She roared and roared and he ran off."

"I heard that he was seen pouring some stuff out of a handkerchief into a rick of hay."

"Go on."

"Foot-and-mouth disease."

"Oh God, help us . . . We're moidered," Mrs. Kelly, the owner of the shop, says, and thanks the gods that at least he has gone. She hears in interrupted snatches how he had the cheek to disguise himself, to knock on the curate's door, to plead hunger in order to get in, and, once in, asked the priest if he had an old pullover and while the priest went upstairs to look made off with the car keys.

"Brand-new car . . . a week old. The poor curate is desperate," Mrs. Kelly said. The group of women fussed over Josie, having heard that the police had raided her house, thinking that he was in it and that she was hostage.

"If you had been, you'd be pulp now," Mrs. Kelly said,

offering her a seat, saying she looked shook, didn't look her old self, didn't look like the lady of the manor at all.

"And you've been having a little holiday?" the postmistress asked.

"Just a few days . . . with my nephew."

"Is he the boy in insurance?"

"Yes, he's in insurance," she says, and wonders why she is lying. How many would understand why she had hidden McGreevy; how many would do it themselves and like her not know why?

She is plied with questions about her time in the nursing home and whether the nuns were nice or demons and what it feels like to be back in her own house again, in her castle.

"You should get good locks . . . Locks on all the doors and all the windows," Mrs. Kelly says, and adds that it is not only the ones who want a free Ireland but ordinary criminals as well, hosts of them.

"Is he married?" a young girl asks.

"Is who married?" Josie asks. She feels estranged from them all, a criminal.

"Your nephew."

"No, but he's engaged," and with each untruth she seems to incriminate herself more.

On the way out, the Guards watch her with binoculars from the barracks window. They have been waiting for her homecoming. Cornelius, a young Guard who is presently going to interview her, beckons to Rory to come and have a look. Rory, who is not local but from a station six miles away, has been collating information because of knowing the environs so well, knowing the woods.

"Are you sure that's her?" he asks Cornelius.

"That's her . . . I went there about a dog licence last year."

"Funny, I thought she'd be different altogether . . . more of a toff. That the nephew?"

"It must be," and they watch as the driver takes the basket of groceries and sacks of turf; stacks them in the boot.

"Give them a few minutes to get home," Rory says, and thinks how peculiar that she had no luggage.

Oh, the dry words, the dry words, and the jousting as they eye one another, she complaining because much of the house had been pillaged and Cornelius showing no consideration at all. A young Guard with the buckle of his belt digging into his flab and his notebook open and two sheets of carbon paper carefully inserted. Pointing to the disorder, the drawers and pictures on the floor, the flittered pages of the antiquarian books stripped of their binding, she has to remind him that this is not how she keeps house; moreover, his comrades have broken her little tortoiseshell music box, so that spasmodically it lets out sputters of sound, thin and tinkly, like glasses stacked too close together on a drinks tray.

"My house is a pigsty," she says, and recalls the floorboards in the spare rooms lifted, mattresses ripped, and the wadding around the springs eerie like witches' tresses. Why they had not rifled her bedroom she would never know. To all of it he is impervious, caught up in his own rhetoric, how everything imaginable constitutes a clue, how miscellaneous evidence is vital, no stone left unturned while looking for cans, containers, rope, wire, fuses, blasting caps, diagrams, anything foreign to the immediate surroundings.

"Except that you found nothing," she says, nerving herself.

"You get a feeling and you stick with it," he says.

"I couldn't believe it when I walked through the door," she says.

"A big old house like this makes Gardai work very complicated," he says, and untops his pen with his teeth. He would like to ask her a few questions.

"Go ahead," she says overcalmly.

A trusted source has mentioned this, another trusted source has mentioned that, so that when she answers he advises that she keep her wits about her.

"My wits," she says sarcastically.

Nothing would make her betray him now. For one thing he has gone. For another she has a revulsion against this youth, the lumpen way he walked across her floor, ignorant of the chaos, and having the gall to welcome her home.

"You are aware?"

"Aware of what?"

"That what you say will be taken as evidence against you."

"Except that I have nothing relevant to say."

"A person who harbours a subversive incurs the responsibility for it."

"You've searched and searched."

"Have you seen this person?" he asks, producing a "Wanted" leaflet on which there are two pictures of McGreevy, one when he was younger, wide-browed and with a head of hair, and the more recent one with thinning hair and his grey moustache, so spare as if it is enamelled onto him. She reads his approximate age, his height, his build, the colour of his eyes, his accent, and the fact that he smokes cigarettes, and she reckons that they got the colour of the eyes wrong.

"No."

"Of course, the presence of such a man might prove an enrichment to a person's life."

"Might it?"

"To a lonely person, such as yourself."

"I take exception to that remark."

"Exception or not, a pattern has been emerging—that he has been in this locality and maybe even in this house."

"Then it's your job to find him."

"The Garda are doing their job and doing it well and doing everything to calm and restore public confidence."

"I can't help you," and she turns, picks up one of the drawers, and tries to wedge it back into the empty socket.

"I haven't finished."

"No?"

"A trusted source has described you as a hermit—would you agree with that?"

"I certainly keep myself to myself, if that's what you mean."

"You play your cards close to your chest, Mrs. O'Meara."

"I need to. You people have the feeling you can walk over folk."

"Have you or have you not seen this man?"

"I don't have a television."

"Good Christ. The whole country is on a red alarm and you seem to know nothing about him—Pollyanna time."

"My nephew mentioned that there was someone on the run."

"Someone! A someone wanted on both sides of the border, for murders and bombings, and this by his own admission; a someone with a very calm exterior given to violent outbursts even in unthreatening situations . . . A madman." He watches as the fear bubbles up in her.

"Who says?"

"A person in his care could be in a liquidiser now."

"Oh please," she says, using the drawer as a breastplate.

"Quite a dangerous cocktail," he says, and whistles to emphasise his anger with her.

"All I want is to be left in peace," she says, trying to be conciliatory now.

"It is incumbent upon me to point out to you that if you have hidden him you will go to prison."

"Prison!" The word too urgent by far. She remembers hoops

of barbed wire running along the length of high walls in a Midland town and how Jamie had said, "Poor buggers in there counting the hours," and how the driver had said no, that they were all doped, that they doped them, to keep them from rioting. Prison. A sprawling mass of mortar and stone with sets of high gates flush upon similar gates, hoop after hoop of barbed wire, the rusted hooks like brown-black maggots rending the air.

"I know you're there." She said the words aloud, not frightened, and as if prompted. She had tidied the kitchen and was eating her supper from a tin. The shopkeeper had made her a gift of the smoked oysters. They were a new thing, a fad, and the doctor's wife had raved about them. She didn't like them, but she ate them anyhow and dipped the shop bread in the savoury yellow oil and sucked on it, as if it was a sponge.

She put the tin down slowly, almost decorously, as the latch was lifted three times, then jerked by what was obviously an unaccustomed hand. In the fading light she was mistaken for an instant, thinking it was him, then saw it wasn't, that the hooded man had a thick crop of black curly hair and workman's hands. He seemed to have no eyes at all, only lids, crusted and pink, and she felt an instant's panic, believing it was someone who had come to settle a score with McGreevy.

"He said to say that if the Guards press you to say you were tied up."

"Who's he?"

"He."

"What else?"

"He said to say he was sorry."

"What else?"

"He needed you to know . . . He hoped you would."

"Sorry for what?"

"I don't know."

But even as he said it, she knew. She knew by the creepiness and the goose pimples that came over her.

"There's something up, isn't there . . . isn't there?" But he is already away, she following, catching up with him around the gable, grasping the sleeve of his anorak.

"He's going to do something . . . That's what the sorry is for, isn't it . . ."

"I don't know. I only pass messages," he says, and breaks loose from her, picking up the bicycle that he has placed flat down on the gravel.

"Oh my God . . . Oh my God," she says, walking back and forth, thinking, not knowing whom she can turn to now. If she tells the police it means he will get killed, and if she doesn't it means that someone else will.

"Do something . . . Do something." Everything, even the silenced clock is saying it.

"There's only one thing," she says, going into the hall to the telephone, thinking how she could have averted all this at the very beginning, washed her hands of him, but no, felt sympathetic, went along with him, for some reason.

"I'm doing something," she said as she picked up the phone and looked for the number on the pad beside it.

"Well . . . he could be . . ." the sister says when asked if her brother Pa is free to do a drive.

"Could be."

"He's having the tay."

"Can you ask him? It's urgent," and while she waits she overhears them laughing and thinks, because such is the insanity of her thoughts, that they are laughing about her.

"When would it be for?" the sister says, returning and still laughing.

"It's for now . . . Now." She is shouting it, irked that the woman has not grasped it already.

"Well . . . sure . . . Being as it's you," she says.

"Tell him I'm ready . . . I'm ready now."

She sits with her hat and coat on and, hearing the phone, goes to it—crestfallen, thinking it is the driver or the sister to say he can't come after all. It is a man's voice, quite educated, quite polished, and as he says her name—"Is this Mrs. O'Meara?"—she grips the ledge and thinks, This is it, this is my executioner.

"Who is that?"

"I'm P.C. Purcell from the station, Rory Purcell, and I wanted . . ."

"Look, I have nothing whatever to tell you. I told the young man all there is to know . . . to know."

"Actually that's why I'm ringing, Mrs. O'Meara, I believe you weren't too pleased with how it went."

"Pleased?"

"They're young lads . . . They're straight out of Tullamore . . . They know nothing about public relations or how to make a person unwind and relax."

"Unwind. I don't need all this trouble, all these questions, at my time of life. Ask the priest, ask the doctor."

"Indeed. That's why I'm ringing, on behalf of the force, to say we're sorry. But you can see yourself how we can leave no stone unturned and how we have your interests at heart, your safety, your well-being."

"I heard in the shop that the person . . . the terrorist has gone."

"You'll hear different things in different shops."

"Do you think he is gone?"

"I'd be surprised . . . I'm iffy about it. I think he's here to do business and we're here to do business with him."

"But once you raided my house, he'd know, wouldn't he?" she says precipitately.

"He needn't know unless someone told him . . . a sympathiser."

"That's true," she says, and flinches, to stop herself saying anything else, yet by her very next remark confirms his hunch that maybe she is implicated.

"I hope for his sake he's gone," she says.

"For his sake. What about the slaughter he might be planning to do?"

"The slaughter." With each word she begins to feel herself falter.

Were that policeman there now, facing her, she would probably tell him; she would probably say, "Yes, he was here. Something about him made me . . . succumb . . . Maybe I didn't believe he could kill or would kill." But while thinking it, she is saying yes to him, agreeing with him as he dilates on the serpentine cunning of these blokes, and eventually she feels calmer, believing that she has extricated herself. Except that she is wrong. He is thinking that his hunch is right, the hunch that made him decide to telephone her, that made him disregard all the blather about the fella taking the curate's car and all the non-evidence from the search, and that he sensed it when he saw her in the town, worried, dishevelled, looking from left to right as if she was being watched.

"By the way, I wanted to ask your nephew a question about his car registration. It bears a striking resemblance to a car that crowd had."

"That wasn't my nephew."

"No?"

"No . . . My nephew was too busy and he got a student to run me."

"Then I'll have to ask the student."

"I'll ask for you."

"Let me have a word with your nephew . . . Save you the bother."

"I'd rather ask him myself . . . Coming from you he might think I'd gone batty."

"That's fine . . . I'll give you a shout tomorrow," he says, and hangs up. The full import of it takes a few seconds as he retraces each line of conversation and thumps himself for not having taped it. One thing is sure: the woman has lied. He has caught her red-handed. There may not even be a nephew. Why has she lied? Where has she been?

"She knows something . . . She knows too much," he says aloud.

"What makes you say that?" Guard Linihan says. He knows the woman, quite standoffish.

"What makes me say it is that she lied. Then got hot and bothered about ringing her nephew, said he'd think his aunt had gone batty."

"If she's a Republican I'm a Mormon."

"Where's her house?" Rory says, walking into the other room, where Cornelius is downing his supper.

"You go through the town, you come to a corner, there's an old forge and a pub . . . Now you can take either the lake road or the road past the creamery."

"Which is quicker?"

"Well, it depends."

"Which road is shorter, Con?"

"The creamery road," and he stands as if he is going to be clouted.

Rory sees her in the back of the car, her face bent forward as she says something to the driver, then sitting back and pulling the brim of her hat down. He thinks and knows in his gut that the alarm is on. No time to get reinforcements yet, no time to do anything, only follow at a sensible distance and see where she is headed for and then decide.

"Oh, little Aoife . . . your daddy's flying now," he says, and drives along and thinks as he always does when there's danger, What beautiful countryside, what serenity, what a beautiful tragic country to be born into.

"Some place," McGreevy says, and stoops as he goes inside the hut. They are already waiting, Brennan flicking on and off a pocket torch and Cassidy the messenger who had been to her house.

"Yes . . . The Fir Bolgs slept here," Brennan says, lifting his hood.

"Were they the men with the big bellies?" Cassidy asks.

"You're late, McGreevy."

"I had to go around two towns."

"What the fuck did you have to take her to the cottage for?"

"You mean the woman?"

"I mean the woman."

"I had nowhere else to take her . . . Her own house was shopped."

"You could have left her there."

"I couldn't let her die."

"What's she done . . . made a will in your favour?"

"They would've questioned her if I brought her back home . . . She might've spilt the beans."

"Bringing her to the cottage was an act of lunacy."

"She didn't know where she was. They're old hands, Creena and her mother."

"I hope they're old hands," he says, and gives him the box. The wind is howling and the loose sheets of galvanise on the roof jig with a vengeance.

"Your Christmas box."

"What for?"

"What feckin' for."

"I was told from above that he's not coming."

"He is fucking coming."

"How do you know?"

"I've been at the start of it . . . My cousin works in the law courts . . . In the canteen."

"I was told it was off, O-F-F."

"That was four days ago."

"You could be out of touch."

"I was warned agin you."

"Oh yeh."

"Bit of an elitist . . . You like to run the show."

"I often think I have to."

"You have a few enemies."

"There are things we do and things we do not do."

"Well, this is one you do do," and thrusts the box at him. It is a tall box, like the Blessed Martin de Pores box that used to be on the school table, and there are lashings of tape around it.

"When did the factor change?"

"Two days ago . . . His doctor gave the okay."

"Are there women with him?"

"A private secretary and a male nurse and a skipper."

"How do we know that's all?"

"Getting yellow, are we?"

"This is your part of the country."

"For the record, it's not my part of the country . . . I'm forty or fifty miles from here."

"It's more your part of the country than mine."

"But it's your assignment," the voice says.

"I was on my way back up . . ."

"Still . . . You wouldn't like to see the chalice pass from you."

"When do they get here?"

"They'll be putting their rods down Friday."

"There's no fishing this time of year." He jumps. A rat has just slithered across his instep, and toppling, he lands in a puddle, thick with water and turgid with turf dust. His boots are like two sods of turf on him now.

"It's not to fish . . . it's to revisit old haunts. He has cancer . . . of the bowel."

"Then he's for it anyhow," he hears himself say.

"Has the woman got to you? How did she do it? Tea and scones or the jukebox?"

"The woman has not got to me."

"I hope you're not cracking."

"Nothing's broken me, ever."

"Only we could do that . . ."

"You don't have to give me that garbage."

"A journeyman like you . . . wouldn't like to be lost to the undertaker." And he goes out, stooped and limping. Impossible to say whether the limp is real or a stunt.

"Look . . . We don't know . . . We don't know and even if we did . . . we wouldn't interfere . . . We couldn't interfere." Creena's mother sits with her hands folded, calm but annoyed that the woman has come on such an impertinent errand.

"But I can't . . . We can't allow it to happen."

"We can. We do. We're not you. We're different from you. We know what they do . . . And we know that they have to do it."

Creena sits to one side, feeling a little embarrassed at having been so fond of the woman and now having to withdraw and be on her mother's side and on McGreevy's side, and on the side of the cause.

"His wife was his comrade," Creena says.

"His wife?"

"She stayed here once. She waited for him here . . . He never came. I remember her waiting all night . . . all night. She said, 'If either of us is to get killed, I'd rather it was me.' She was killed three days after . . . She knew it was coming . . . She could feel it was coming. She was killed nursing the child."

"Oh, the poor woman."

"She loved him . . . She believed in him."

"Everyone loves him. But doesn't believe in what he's doing."

"We do . . . We do," the mother says. By her standing up she is also saying, "For your own sake and for ours, go back home; this is no night to be here, and this is no night to have you here."

"We'd love to have you at Christmas," Creena says, and from the font gives her a drop of holy water.

"Did anyone see you come?" the mother asks.

"Only the driver . . . He's down at the road."

"See her down the bohereen," the mother says to Creena, but she does not signal the woman goodbye.

After they have shot two rats, they reckon that the others have scarpered out of fright. Cassidy has had the job to kick the dead ones out with his boot.

"I wonder if dogs eat them . . . Fur an' all."

"You went to the house?" McGreevy says, looking at him through the binoculars.

"Yeh."

"What did you say?"

"What you said to say."

"What did you say?"

"That you said sorry."

"And?"

"She ran after me . . . She said, 'Something's up, isn't there . . . He's going to do something, he's going to do something terrible, that's why he's saying sorry.' "

"Jesus . . . The fat's in the fire," McGreevy says, and puts the binoculars in the hole above the lookout.

"What'll I tell Brennan?"

"Tell him . . ."

"Where are you going?"

"Tell him anything."

"He's a hard man, he is. I know something he did . . . He asked a guy that he was suspicious of to come and see him, and he brought him out into a field where he had dug a grave . . . He shot the guy into his own grave. Cool."

"This job is jinxed."

"He meant what he said, Mac."

"I've never not slept before."

" 'Twill be all over Friday."

"Or won't be," he says, his nerviness laid bare for an instant before he goes out. If he quit and ran now, what would he do, what was there?—nothing else, nothing else. His life was graphed by others and his deeds punished or rewarded by others, but that was not why he did it; it was his oath to himself, made long ago, drunk at the breast.

"So it's on."

"I'll meet you where I said I'd meet you," he says, as taciturn as that.

"I want every squad car there is. It's two miles beyond this telephone kiosk on the left side . . . Up a small bohereen

. . . There's a big tree . . . I mean there's two big trees looped together at the corner." His voice is rough, rapid, his only fear being that Manus is not grasping it and will not act fast enough.

"What kind of trees?"

"Oak, beech . . . Get a move on, Manus. Mobilise, mobilise."

"Shouldn't I ring Dublin first . . . ring the super in charge?"

"You can ring Dublin later."

"He's in charge."

"I'm running it now . . . Ring every station within a twenty-mile radius . . . Get every squad car there is . . . Quick . . . Assemble . . . Mobilise . . . Move."

"Will I come?"

"No . . . You're a veteran. You stay put."

In the cottage the two women confront him, smirks on their faces, as if they had been expecting him.

"Who's been here?" Rory asks.

"No one's been here."

"You had no visitors?"—to which they both shake their heads.

"What about the lady in the long coat?"

"If you know, why ask?"

"Look, Mrs. Burke, you had better cooperate. I know she was here . . . I saw her come and I saw her go. Now, why was she here?"

"A social call."

"She didn't stay long."

"She didn't feel well."

"If she didn't feel well, why didn't she phone and say she wasn't coming?"

"Because you lot have our telephone tapped."

"Get your hat and coat on, both of you," he says.

"Oh, are we going to the pictures?" Creena asks.

"Get your hat and coat on," he says, and as he does, the mother hears the sirens starting up in the valley down below and knows that yes, the woman was right, the woman was right about its being a fateful night on the mountain. Instinctively she sprinkles holy water first on her daughter, then on herself, then on the floor, making sure to avoid where he stands.

"We love our country," she says contemptuously.

"So do we all," he says.

"If you did, you wouldn't be doing this," she says. The sight of a man in uniform is a repetition of what happened twenty years back; her husband dragged in on a halter from the bog, a Guard in front of him and a Guard behind him and a car waiting for him, and his asking if he could have a word with his wife and not being allowed, and her standing there, watching him go, waving, her little Creena a mite inside her belly, watching him being carted off, because he loved his country.

"Oh feck and feck." Brennan hears the sirens and knows that his number is up. The mountain is alive with them, sirens in long breath-holding shrieks, following one upon another, answering each other, signalling the sweet resolute Morse of vengeance. Cars are coming in every direction so that he cannot loop back, all he can do is get on. McGreevy, the bastard, the tout. All of it making sense now, the demur, the showing up late, the wanting to pass the chalice. Oh feck and feck. From high up on the prow of the mountain, he sees the Ford coming towards him, puts his foot down, and reckons he can block them and wipe them out as they come round the hairpin bend.

"Get down . . . Get down, Ned," Tom says to the young Guard who is driving. It is the first time in his life that his actions precede his thoughts; he has already jerked the bolt and fired from the moving car at the figure whose vehicle straddles the road. The figure, hooded and armed, is on the bonnet, firing. Getting out of the car, he crouches, uses a boulder as cover, then opens fire, his bullets and the opposing bullets singing in the startled twilight, the shells pitching onto things, yellow flame and black smoke, the whine of the ricochets, and no backup car yet to help him through. The guy is shouting. He does not know whether he is asking to give up or whether it is a trick.

"Drop your gun," he shouts back, his voice lost in the oncoming hammering, and hoping and praying now that his chamber will not give out, he rises, rushes it, and sprays the bonnet of the car as if someone, someone, is impelling him to do it. He sees an arm go down and something float off like a big bird, and he thinks that's his hood and realises that the man is down. That's all he knows, that the man is down. The sudden silence is appalling.

"Did you get him?" Ned asks, crawling towards him, saliva spilling out of his mouth.

"I don't know." He starts to reload, filling it by feel, because darkness has suddenly descended. Moving across he sees the body slumped over the car but twitching, twitching, and he thinks, If I have to shoot point-blank, then I'll have to shoot point-blank. The ebbing of the life, even in that darkness, was like seeing an electric current fizzling out, the jigging getting less and less, then nothing, only a heap, a still heap, and looking in over him he hears nothing, least of all a breath.

"I got him," he says to Ned, who is trembling beside him.

"We should say an act of contrition."

"You say it," he says, and hauls the body down to lay it on the bank. It feels light, innocuous, the back a warm pallet of shedding blood. It is too dark to see where the bullet went and he is glad of that, glad that he cannot see. Something, shame or pity, makes him take off his jacket to cover the chest and the face.

The cars and sirens screaming up the hill towards them let out their incessant and revelrous cry, and he thinks, They'll crash through us . . . They'll kill us all, and jumping up and pulling off his shirt, he starts to wave it wildly to alert them.

A sergeant whom he doesn't know, seeing him half naked and waving, mistakes him for an instant and cocks a pistol.

"I'm a Guard," he shouts, and then in a voice less frenzied, "I've just shot one of them."

"Good work," the sergeant says as he gets out and orders the convoy behind to get past somehow, to get up on the ditch, to ram the car that's blocking the road, and as they're doing it Ned has the task of dragging the warm corpse out of the way, to save it from being pulped to bits.

"We'll get an ambulance over here," the sergeant says, getting into his own car.

"And a priest," Ned says as they whiz past him, the sounds inhuman, the shapes of the vehicles like meteors, bounding and bouncing over the mountain pass.

"I'll have to get word to my wife," Tom says. "I'll have to go and phone," and he points to a lighted window a distance away, in from the road.

"I'll go," Ned says. He'd rather not be alone with the dead man. It was bad enough hearing the firing, seeing the gun muzzle jump, but to be alone with him is woeful.

"No, I'll have to tell her myself," Tom says, and as he runs he starts to put on his shirt.

Two huge dogs leap out and make for his trouser leg, while inside the house a curtain is lifted but the door is not opened in answer to his knocking or his call. At the window he appeals to the owner, puts his hands up in a gesture of desperation.

"I'm a Guard," he says as the window is opened a fraction, but the man does not believe him.

"Show me your identification," the voice says.

"There's been a shooting on the road," he says.

"I'm not letting you in otherwise . . ."

Rooting in his pocket he finds the plastic card with his photo and his rank.

Inside, children are herded into a group, staring at him like children at a horror picture.

"Bandit country . . . bandit country," the man is saying. There seems to be no wife.

"It's not our fault that it's bandit country," he says. He's been through hellfire and not a single human being has asked him how he is. He knows that they're listening on the phone. That doesn't help, and neither does his wife's voice, cold and impersonal when he tells her that there's been a serious incident and a guy is shot.

"Did you shoot him?" she asks.

"It was me did it," he says, pausing, expecting a breath of sympathy.

"I'll tell the children," she says.

"Don't . . . I'll break it to them," he says flatly.

"They might hear it otherwise . . . It might be on the news."

"Don't turn on the bloody news," he says, hurt that she has not said, "How are you?" or, "Is there anyone by your side?" On the way out the man approaches him for money for the telephone call.

"Bandit country," he says, and tosses the coin onto the stove.

The cars swing through the open gate, swerving wildly to make room for one another as they surround the cottage. Many, believing that McGreevy is in there, leap over steps and rockery, sending hens and geese, pots of flowers in all directions, overwhelming the two beagles, who can do nothing but growl.

"Would you mind not stepping all over my flowers," Mrs. Burke shouts out.

"Search the house," Rory says as he sees them file in.

"They'll ruin the new carpet," Creena says.

"It's the kicking down of a rotting door, Miss Burke," Rory says, and gestures the men to get moving. A colleague coughs and beckons him out and he realises that something has happened, something big.

"We got one of them."

"McGreevy . . ."

"Not McGreevy. The Limerick sergeant thinks that it's a guy called Brennan . . . He recognised him by an iron hand."

"Dead?"

"He'll never father a child again."

"Who hit?"

"Tommy Conlon."

"Tommy Conlon . . . The Quiet Man . . . Is he all right?"

"He seems all right . . . He's down at the turn where it happened. There's a boy with him . . . They're waiting for the priest and the ambulance."

"Good work . . . We've got one. Now we want the others . . . We want the whole pack of them," and he runs to recall the officer who is leaving with the two women.

"Put them in separate cells. They mustn't be allowed to talk to anyone. I want the whole thing kept secret . . . Not a word about a man being killed . . . Nothing to the press . . . Tell Manus. Absolute secrecy . . . Lids on."

"Manus said what about the woman in the big house?"

"Don't hit the woman yet. I want a surveillance on the house. Get the night spots . . . Something's cooking there."

"Manus says Dublin is put-out."

"Tell Manus to tell Dublin that this is cowboy country and we're cowboys here."

In the torch light he sees something to give him thought—an old headboard filling up a gap, but so plaited with briars and furze as to seem out of the ordinary.

"Where does that track lead to?" he shouts, leaning into the car, where the two women are conversing with galling calm.

"Nowhere," Creena says insolently.

"Good," he says back to her. "If you say nowhere, that means somewhere," and hurries back to pick his team.

"Michael, you're a young Turk, you go up that track and see what there is to see and report back to me."

"If I see one of them," Michael says, too abashed to say, "I don't want to go . . . I don't want to go alone."

"Get me on the radio . . . We'll be up."

Turning towards the house he picks the first two men he sees. No time to waste. The mountain could be crawling with them.

"You and you," he says roughly. The heavier man, Tobin, winks at his colleague, Duggan, and says under his breath, "It's his show," and they follow him halfheartedly and stand beside the furze-filled headboard, which is lying flat on the ground.

"Pure madness," Tobin says as they wait. The dark, a god-forsaken path, and now clouds bursting apart and rain on their heads and rain on their uniforms and rain that will make a muddy track impassable.

As he waits for a signal from Michael, Rory whispers into his radio, repeating the same thing: "One, two, three, over, Michael," and curses at not getting a response.

"No shots anyhow," Duggan whispers as they wait.

"There's other ways of killing a man besides shooting him . . . There's the knife," Tobin says.

"We'll have to go up," Rory says.

"This is a bollocks . . . We shouldn't be doing this," Tobin says, and stands as if he might refuse to go.

"How should we be doing it?"

"We should have a team of men . . . helicopters."

"We have no alternative and you know that," Rory says, and starts ahead.

Silhouetted in the distance is a figure, or what looks like a figure that might even be a tree, and fixing it as best he can, Rory aims his gun and moves towards it, ready to cap it.

"Halt." It's Michael's voice, very unassured.

"Fuck's sake, Michael," Rory calls back, hoarse.

"What's up there?"

"There's a hut on the spur of the mountain."

"Is there cover?"

"There's only what you can see."

"You go first, Michael . . . I'm behind you . . . Then you . . . Then you."

"Utter bollocks," Tobin says again.

The wind has risen now, steady and raw, driving rain against their faces and into their eyes, against their frames, as they strive to balance on the muddy path, which as it gets steeper becomes slipperier, with here and there roots of gorse bushes, flung down into it, to take the rains.

"It's rugged," Duggan says.

"Rugged, it's perpendicular," Tobin says, and stands and wheezes.

"C'mon now," Rory calls. He moves so fast it is as if he is above the ground in some rhythmic prance, like a pony, a reserve of strength that he keeps for times like this.

"What's that?" Michael says. The wind circulating in the

bracken was like the movement of a crouched man or an animal in there.

"Nothing," Rory says and slaps him fondly to urge him on, then from behind hears a "Holy Moses" as Tobin trips and falls.

"Help me . . . Help me," Tobin shouts.

"Fuck's sake . . . You're on a job . . . Lives depend on it," Rory says, but waits until the man gets up to make sure that he can walk.

"I tripped."

"Well, don't trip," Rory says, and hurries on ahead to catch up with Michael, whose eagerness is getting the better of him, just as his trembling had a while before. He stands and convenes the four of them by a tree, the only vestige of nature up there.

"If anything goes wrong . . . come back here to this spot."

"Maybe we won't be able to come back to this spot," Duggan says matter-of-factly.

"This is your rendezvous . . . Come back to it," he says bluntly.

"It's a thorn tree . . . They're not lucky," Michael says, but almost to himself.

"We're together in this . . . You hear shooting and you're the only one, don't try to be a hero . . . And don't shoot one another," he says, by way of giving them a bit of courage.

As they approach it, he sees it not so much in outline as by a bulk, darker, solider than the surrounding dark, a hut without animals and miles from everywhere.

"You cover for us," he says, dispatching the men to either side, while Michael and he go on up, so tensed now they are scarcely breathing.

"Stay close to me, Michael, all the time," he whispers.

"How close?"

"About ten feet."

They wait then for the other two men to take their positions, and touching Michael on the shoulder, he gives him one last bit of advice: "If you have to shoot, make sure you have a clean line of fire."

"I only had a week of it in training."

"Michael, don't think of that now. Let's go for it . . . I go down . . . you go forward . . . You go down . . . I go forward. If someone starts shooting, shoot back. When we get within twenty feet, you get down and you stay down . . . I'll take the hut . . . alone."

"Are you sure?"

"I'm sure. You cover the door and I'll go in," and then seizing the moment that he knows can lead to anything, a hail of bullets, a booby trap, anything, he kicks the door, and from behind, with Michael shining the torch, he sees the turf floor, a bit of sacking hanging, and a youth fast asleep under the makeshift window.

Cassidy sits up, holding his fly, thinking it is McGreevy and that he will have to find an excuse for nodding off. Feeling the strange face breathing in over him, he reaches for his gun, but in the dark his arm is impeded with a paralysing grasp.

"Get in here, Michael, fast . . . fast," Rory shouts, and presently in the full light from the torch he sees a burly, butty fellow with a thick crop of black hair and he lets out an involuntary "Shit," disappointed that it is not McGreevy.

"Who are you . . . What are you doing here? What organisation do you belong to?" Rory says, hauling him up.

"*Ni Tuigim Bearla*," the voice says.

"Oh Jesus . . . One of the Patrick Pearse fraternity," Rory says, and asks Michael to use his Irish.

"I don't know much."

Fearless now, Cassidy pelts them with a barrage of slogans

and poetry and patriotism, knowing by his fluency and his disdain that he is letting them see that he is a far better keeper of the country's soul and the country's heritage.

"Ni Fuinim, ni tá blasmaireact orainn Uar an Bas . . . On mbrug. Sin meadba go Fained greine ar fairge."

"What the fuck is he saying?"

"He's going too fast for me . . . something about Queen Maeve."

"Tell him he's going too fast for you."

"Ta tu," Michael says, but cannot think of the word for fast, and anyhow he is embarrassed and overpowered by Cassidy, who is telling him that they are all shits, touts, maggots, informers, slaves, and that they should draw their pay packet under the Union Jack and not the Tricolour.

"What is he saying?"

"He's cursing us."

"Ask him why he's carrying that baby," Rory says, pointing to the gun.

"He says he doesn't have to answer that."

"Tell him from me whether he talks or doesn't talk, his grammar and his philology and his cover are up the spout."

"Bas no Onoir." Cassidy shouts it again and again, spitting it into their faces and then hailing through the window hole to the wet and savage countryside beyond.

"What's that?"

"Death or glory," Michael translates.

"Take him out . . . Put the cuffs on him. Duggan and you, bring him down to the station and make sure he doesn't turn into a leprechaun on the way."

Alone he does the search, and in that quick taut series of seconds their strategy reveals itself to him—a pair of binoculars, a heap of stones where the wall was recently hacked, a lookout to the long, low, uninterrupted sweep of heather and bracken, hurtling down, down to the lake, several miles below.

"The lake is the target . . . The target is on the lake," he says, and taps his chest and with exultance shouts for Michael. He has to do a house-to-house search and a boat-to-boat.

"I'll go down with one of them. You stay here."

"What did you find?"

"The lake is the target."

"How do you know?"

"I'll tell you tomorrow . . . Come on out."

"Out?"

"Yes . . . Watch from the outside and keep your light down, and whatever you do, don't come in here again."

"Why not?"

"The most dangerous time is now."

"Now?"

"Yes, the minute I kicked that door open I might have set off a booby trap and in the next few minutes the whole little edifice could go up in smoke."

"Oh my God," Michael says, and blesses himself as they hurry out.

"So he's gone down to civilisation, while we risk our lives up here in the wilderness," Duggan says.

"He has guts, though," Michael says, and remembers how Rory went in, without fear, without undue haste, with a kind of cheer, quiet as a panther. The rain soaking into him does not bother him now; he thinks the night and the danger have made him braver, he thinks he's not the same Michael as went up there, quaking and not knowing a blasted thing, not even knowing how booby traps worked.

"He has guts . . . I want to have his kind of guts," he says, and Duggan does not answer.

It is raining and blowing on the roadside, plashings of rain dropping down on the boulders and on the two men, the wind with a sinister wail in it, the last thing Tom wants to hear. He feels clammy and cold by turns. The aftermath. The shock. He cannot take his jacket back. As soon as the ambulance comes and the priest, they'll be out of here, and the first thing they'll do is stop in the town and have a brandy.

"They should be here soon," Ned says, for something to say, and thinks that maybe the priest's car cannot get by with the squash of cars on the road.

"It gives you the creeps," Tom says, walking, standing, listening.

"You were great to get him."

"Luck. Pure luck."

"The mountain has never known such activity. God, it was tremendous . . . That hail of fire . . ."

"They kept well in," Tom says, pointing to the lit low-lying windows scattered throughout the mountain, their lights merry and festive, like Christmas candles beaming in the grey-black dismal sphere.

"Christmas is no length away," Ned says.

"Don't," Tom says. He isn't able to think beyond what has happened and the fact that there are two men pacing and another up in a ditch, his outsides at least being washed clean in an extreme unction of rain.

"Your man nearly ate me," he says, looking towards that house, describing his knocking on the door, the faces in the window, having to produce his identity before being let in, the children staring at him like children at a horror film.

"Was he a foreigner?"

"No, he wasn't a foreigner," he says bitterly.

"Did you ever see a rigor mortis?" Ned asks, thinking that maybe the dead body is freezing up in the cold.

"Shut up," Tom says, and runs as if he can run from the

scene of it and the craziness of it and the further craziness that out of the twenty Guards called it had to be him, him who never shot anybody in his life.

"Come back, come back," Ned says, running after him.

"Talk to me about anything else, anything else in the world," Tom says.

"Okay," Ned says, but thinks, I don't know what his interests are, whether they're dogs or horses or fishing or women, and all of a sudden and surprising even himself, he starts to recite a school poem, his voice high-pitched and artificial:

They left his blossom white and slender
Beneath Glasneven's shaking sod.
His spirit passed like sunset splendour
Unto the dead Fianna's God.

Good luck be with you, Michael Collins,
Or stay or go you far away;
Or stay you with the folk of fairy
Or come with ghosts another day.

"*Beal na blát*—The Mouth of the Flowers," he says.

"The mouth of the flowers," Tom says, and wonders what flowers they were and thinks maybe bog lilies, yellow and blue, bog lilies.

"There'll be a poem about this soon," Ned says.

"Oh Jesus," Tom says, opening his mouth wide intending to scream, but it was not as a scream it came out, but quiet and grave and anguished—"No . . . I am not all right and I will never be all right," and going over he whips the jacket off the dead man, and looking down at the perpetually asleep features, he says in a whisper as if only to be heard by the three of them, says in a broken voice, "Half of you hopes you got him and the other half hopes you didn't," and then he puts the jacket back, and the slow sad guttural drops in the aftermath of rain fall onto it, like softly tempered funeral gongs.

"I know . . . I'd be the same . . . We're all Irish under the skin," Ned says, quiet.

"They say a thing like this finishes you. One of the three big Ds . . . Drugs . . . Drink . . . Divorce."

"I think I hear the priest now," Ned says, and goes towards the turn where a car has stopped.

"Father . . ." It is Tom who speaks first, hoping to be absolved. He is an elderly priest, and the wind flaps under his cassock and lifts the cloth that is covering the cup of holy oils.

"Where are the remains?" the priest says curtly.

"He's here."

"This country is wiping itself out."

Tom could not be sure what he meant, or to whom he referred, himself or the shape sprawled pitifully and harmlessly against the sodden ditch.

"I'll need some light."

"We have no light . . . We weren't expecting a thing like this," he says harshly, and so they have to make do with the flicker of match after match, a blaze so brief, so immediately dampened, that he does not have to see the face or the throat onto which the drops of oil are being placed. He would never see the face properly; he had not seen it when they tried to slay one another in the crossfire and he does not see it now, match after match sputtering out in the wet and the Latin murmur of the prayers so very incongruous to a man whose death was still an ignorance to those belonging to him. Who were they? Who would miss him? Who would bury him?

It was as they went down the road towards their car that he gripped Ned. A figure started out of the bushes, then walked slowly towards him, and for a moment he thought he was one of them, come for revenge. Before he could even think, the figure gripped his arm, mashed it, and said: "I'm proud of you

. . . I'm proud of what you did for Ireland this night," and then he disappeared into the pockets of darkness, and for all they knew the man was a ghost or a phantom come to give them heart.

"Who do you think he was?" Tom said.

"A shepherd . . . Weird."

"I always heard that this part of the county held the powers of darkness in it."

"Spirits and things."

"And it was our luck to drive up into it."

"You and I should keep in touch, Tommy," Ned says.

"Oh, we will," Tom says.

He could only guess at the trouble and disjunction which lay ahead, a blighted family life, cold sweats in the night, and the phone calls: "We know who you are and we'll get you." And maybe they would.

"Do you hear it?" she says. She says it to herself and is both teller and listener. It is a wild wind, a warning wind, a wind cooked up by the Furies. It races around the house, each gust followed by another and another, destruction in its howl—things clatter along the yard, a bucket, a bit of fallen gutter, something heavier, a chimney pot, all swept away in its belly. The sound is at once high and low, signalling two different outcomes.

"Yes," she says to a knock on her door. He does not come in. He is not even there. She peers out into the hall where on the bamboo table the artificial tea roses and an Infant of Prague statue unite in shiver.

"Mac," she calls, but he does not answer. She looks through the landing window then and believes that the roots of the cedar tree are being sucked from their holdings. It will fall forward and damage the house, the tree which her husband believed was guarding it. The tops of the evergreens are doing battle with each other, then sinking into one another's clutches. Where was McGreevy now? How many more fields would he cross until they caught up with him? The picture she willed was of him walking forever and ever in the dark of night, wet, wintery, slobbery night, because in that way he could come to no harm and he could wreak none.

Sitting on her bed with the light on, she thinks the sheets of glass in the windowpane will come undone. She watches each one sway, wondering which of the twelve hand-blown gooseberry-coloured panes will be the first to succumb. The north window is taking the brunt of the wind better and she divides her time studying both.

The door flies open, and thinking now that he has come, she bunches the counterpane around herself and walks to meet him. It is while she is saying his name that the lights fuse and now both dark and balk send her hurrying to search the house. In the passage as she shields the candle flame her hand looks exceedingly large and clumsy to her, like a man's hand. The room he occupied is as empty and forlorn as it was a few hours earlier, a ghost room, and yet his presence is somewhere in it, like a haw on a window.

The tears, the ones that the nurse had told her to allow to fall, come pouring out as she sits on his bed and thinks he should have left a note with Creena, should have said goodbye, and she keeps seeing him, especially his hands, washed and rewashed, pinkish against his sandy face as he raised them to recollect himself in answer to some question of hers or to retreat from her. Her mind is made up about one thing. She will give the house over to young people, a youth hostel for those who travel, a place to be lived in. Is it he, is it he that has made her decide that, or is it the night? It is not the night.

The sound of his feet, his boots, his anorak, and, even in candlelight, something aghast in his expression.

"Did I frighten you?" he says.

"I thought you'd . . . you'd . . ."

"It's a shocking night."

"But you're back."

"I'll be gone in a day or two."

"I got frightened. I began to imagine things . . . Things," she says, but decides not to elaborate, not to tell him that she had gone back to the cottage to enquire about his movements.

"I've probably caught pneumonia."

"Let me make you a warm drink."

"No, I'll sleep. I'll sleep it off."

"Creena and her mother were very kind."

"They are."

"They . . . told me . . . something of your . . . life. How you lost your wife."

"I did."

"How—she was shot."

"She was."

"And that the child she was nursing clung on to her bracelet."

"It did."

"Was that when you panicked?"

"No. That was not when I panicked," he says, and then something despite himself makes him tell it, how he was asleep in the cell, how the governor and the warders could not waken him, how they broke his door down at dawn and yet he did not believe it, thought it was one of their lies, and how he asked them to bring a radio, heard it then, heard it on the six o'clock news after the pips, how his wife, aged thirty, was slain by two masked men.

"Good God, how awful."

"It is . . . But it's the quality of a life that counts," he says quietly.

"Why would you think they were lying in the prison?"

"They were always testing you . . . They were always trying to break you. That was the intention."

She reaches as if she might touch him, just this once, and seeing it he shifts, then turns away and takes out a cigarette. Everything is getting to him, the boundaries of his night askew, Brennan with his undertaker talk, the storm, and now the woman, shivering, and these questions, these questions.

"And then you lost your little girl?"

"Yes."

"What was her name?"

"Kitty." Kitty. Halting, abbreviated, as if he grudged to say it.

"I came down here . . . I . . . I was unsettled . . . The storm, the young man that you sent and the empty house," she says, still hoping that he will turn round.

"There's good ghosts here."

"I hope so— What did your little girl die of?"

"Her heart gave out."

"Were you with her?"

"No, she was with a relative."

"Were you a good parent?"

"I hope I was," he says, and brings his hands up to his eyes as if to say, Oh, please let her not ask me things, let her not wring out of me what belongs solely to me, let her not push open doors that I myself have not seen and must one day see and stand on either side of.

"I'll be off in a day or two," he says again, to appease her. But it is not that she wants. It is not that at all. Why the trembling, why the catch in his voice, where has he been, has he been to see his comrades, those dark and hooded people, have they met and plotted in some ordinary house, with a kettle boiling, or maybe not in some ordinary house, but in some dump? Has something happened?

"Talk to me . . . Talk." She is pleading now.

"Sometimes I can't talk . . . I just can't."

"If you left . . . your . . . organisation . . . would you . . ."

"There would be another to take my place and another after him. That's us."

"I pray," she says.

"Don't . . . There's enough people praying for me already," he says, the voice sharp, sarcastic, abrupt.

Taking the candle from the little table she hurries out.

"You done a lot for me . . . You done a lot for me," he calls, but she does not look back.

His eyes are misted over and he has never felt so cold in all his life. What want in him has brought him back? Why hadn't he stayed in that shed, with Cassidy and the rats, beside the thing, working it out in his mind, every thread and fibre of it, the coiled silence of it, a duplicate of himself?

Brocades and velvets seem not the ravelled relics they are but things of beauty, and old cracked Toby jugs and shepherdesses have taken on a lustre, enshrined in the dreaming haziness of lamplight. The dust rises and sidles, the motes gold-flecked, the fire lit, holly along the mantel, a Christmasy feeling in the big room and rugs to put over their knees.

Twice in the day she knocked, having left tea and eats, and the third time she peeped in and saw him as she had not ever seen him, defenceless and muttering and insignificant. He had changed his lair to the shoe closet and lay under a shelf, doubled up, shoes and must all around him. After dark she asked him to come out.

"It's very peaceful," Cormac says. By that he means that a hole in the ground with briars and bushes above them, a wet corner of a boulder as a seat and eight or nine hours of surveillance ahead of them, is not a hectic way to spend a winter's night.

"Nice moon," he says sometime later. Something about Matt, his superior, makes him say these idiotic things. A moon is no help to them at all. Bright moonlight is not what they want, but darkness, darkness in order to get a clearer picture of what's going on inside the house.

"You can keep your moonlight," Matt says, and positions the telescope so that he can look through it without having to move it again. He warns about not touching it unnecessarily, says any piece of machinery can let you down.

"They're good yolks," Cormac says, eager to touch it.

"They're better than what you have at the races," Matt says, and then leans back, allowing Cormac to look through it, to get the hang of it. What he sees is a room somewhat blurry, like the snow inside a paperweight, only green, everything green.

"Do you think he's there?" Cormac asks in a whisper.

"Your guess is as good as mine."

"He wouldn't be mad enough to come back to the place."

"Mad people do mad things," Matt says.

"Why is everything green?" Cormac wonders.

"Turn the fecking thing off . . . No point in wasting the battery . . . We'll need it."

"Do you think we will?"

"With the help of God we will."

They sit side by side, Matt pushing his elbows out like oars, positioning and repositioning himself to get the space and the comfort he requires. Young lads have to learn to be accommodating and to shrink themselves in tight surroundings.

"I hear he's a very quiet sort of person. A prison guard in an interview said he was a model prisoner . . . Made no trouble at all . . . Did the sewing for the others, sewed on buttons and patched their jeans."

"Yeah, and arranged for a power cut in the town and a ton of explosives to be brought in on a digger so that he could make his getaway."

"What happened?"

"What happened! He was apprehended in the dark."

"A teacher was cracked about him."

"Will you stop fecking yapping."

"Sorry."

In the silence they can hear cows grazing, the soft steady cropping of grass and sometimes a wheeze or a moan.

"Sorry, Matt," Cormac says after what seems an age. He likes the man, wants the man to like him, knows he was second choice for the job because of Eamon going down with flu.

"Ah, it's me . . . I'm always uptight on these jobs," Matt says, and by way of amends points to the flask of soup and says gruffly, "Have a slug of that."

"Eamon would have been better," Cormac says shyly.

"Are you telling me you'd rather not be here?"

"I don't know."

"Go on . . . admit it . . . You like the buzz."

"I suppose I do. But I know fellas that would rather be in rooms studying and swotting."

"Don't I know them well . . . Eejits . . . Getting promoted in no time. They'd pass out on one of these jobs . . . Wouldn't be able for it at all. They're a bag of theories . . . The Road Traffic Act and God knows what other Act . . . They know them by heart—oh yes, the miscellaneous forms of trace evidence, the characters of kleptomaniacs, the questions to ask when a bomb is reported: 'When is the bomb going to explode, where is it right now, what does it look like, what kind of bomb is it?' Bollocks."

"You're a gas, man," Cormac says, and thinks things are getting better and that he will taste the soup.

"Then of course there is the caller's voice—is it calm, nasal, angry, excited, rasping, cracking, distinct, slurred, and so on; when all one needs is to get out there and catch the buggers and then find out what kind of voice they had."

"Still, the ones who study a lot get promotion."

"Sure do. But put them at close range and they'd fail to perform. No aptitude . . . none whatsoever."

"I'm always afraid I'll fail."

"Ah . . . You have it in you, you have belly, Cormac."

"Thanks. Thanks, Matt," and then he says it to himself, then dares to say it aloud: "I wonder if he's the desperado they say he is."

"Well, he's not Santa Claus."

"I had a girlfriend from the North and she saw awful things . . . She was in a car with a guy going to a dance and they were stopped and he was pulled by the hair, dragged half out the window . . . Then taken out and kicked and beaten and left for dead. When she went back next day to report it, she was told that there was no patrol car on that road at that time of night."

"Oh, it's open warfare up there and it's half open warfare down here," Matt says, and undoes the flask and pours into the plastic cup.

"After you."

"Go on . . . You're frozen . . . You're shivering."

"Aren't you cold?"

"This jacket is like an incubator."

"I was admiring it."

"Do you know how much it cost? Three hundred smackers."

"God."

"You'll have one when you've done twenty-odd years."

"Is it green or black?" Cormac asks, touching it.

"It's green to blend in with the forestry and foliage."

"Is it hot?"

"Steaming . . . I'm not going to get my backside wet at my time of life."

"Sound," Cormac says, and praises the soup before he has even touched it.

"Are you hungry?"

"I'm always hungry. I was in a hotel not so long ago and I had lamb with sauce Provençal."

"What were you doing there?"

"I was at a fashion show."

"Cripes."

"There was raspberry dressing on the lettuce and the custard was burnt on top . . . Deliberately. Is your wife a good cook?"

"Good plain cooking."

"That's the ticket."

"Cormac, you're a nice boy, but I sometimes think you're not all there. What in feck's name were you doing at a fashion show?"

"My sister made me . . . She wanted to make the compere jealous."

"Jesus, I haven't felt like that in years."

"She's in Germany now. She married an Englishman . . . a soldier. My mother and father were put out. They didn't say anything, but they didn't laugh at the wedding and they didn't smile in the group photograph."

"Worse if she married one of these maniacs that we're tracking," Matt says, and gestures to Cormac that it is time to have a look.

He sees something. What he sees is a blur, like the snow whirling round inside a paperweight, and a figure come into view.

"I see someone."

"Go on."

"A body . . . a moving body."

"You ape . . . Two arms . . . Two legs and a head," Matt says, and pushes him aside. The woman, her hair unbraided, puts an object, a lamp, on the table, then crosses to draw the shutters. He curses, then exhales pleasantly as only one half of the shutters gets pulled. She sits on a low armchair, her knees down as if in semi-genuflection, like a woman awaiting news from the Angel Gabriel.

"Looks as if she's going to have company," he says.

"Can I look?" Cormac says, thrilling to the fact that they have got something.

"Well, at least she's not tied up," he says, mesmerised by the fact that he can take in the features of the room so clearly.

"She's not tied up because she's a willing accomplice."

"Odd."

"Not odd . . . macabre," Matt says, and strains to see if there is anything more.

"But if you'd been in 1916 you'd be on their side."

"That's different. That's a totally different ball game . . . These guys are without conscience, without ideals, and with only one proclamation, money and guns and murder, guns and money."

"It's a sad thing, all the same."

"It's monstrous. Think of the deaths, the mutilations, the broken families, the gutted homes. You and me and the lads down here risking our lives . . . Think of that."

"The ones that were on hunger strike, though, had a tough time. The Pope sent them a message."

"Evil men, Cormac . . . evil men," Matt says, taking a huge bite from a sandwich, then a second voracious bite before he has had a chance to chew.

"Do you think it will die out?"

"The only thing that will quiet these gurriers is for the ordinary people to say, Enough. Ordinary people get roped in . . . They get frightened . . . They get threatened. They yield to the terror of the vermin."

Cormac balks at the word. At home in Kerry there is a green-and-gold painting of the heroes of 1916, and he can see it, scorched from the flames and a bit smoky, and remembers being picked up as a child and asked to recite the list of names and being praised for it.

"Oh Jesus . . . He's in the room . . . I knew it. Lads telling me he was up the mountain . . . He's in the room . . . He's in the fecking room," Matt says, the confined space of the lime kiln and his uniform too stifling for him as he grabs the radiophone and speaks rapidly, his voice halfway between speech and song.

"Tango, one two three, over." He shouts it.

"I want to see him," Cormac says, and crawls in under the straps, then eases himself up so that he can look at the legend, the Cúchulainn, and what he sees is a man smaller than himself standing in the middle of the room, in short sleeves, hesitant in the midst of such grandeur.

At first he refuses the drink, says it is against orders, and relents only after she has coaxed him by saying that it is unlucky for her to drink alone. Moreover, it is harmless, cloves in hot water with a splash of port. The glasses are so blisteringly hot they cannot hold them. He exhales on his, but keeps looking at her, a boyish, tentative look, to make sure it is not inappropriate. She is looking at his hip. He is not carrying a gun. Out of deference, she reckons. His body, which she has never studied before, looks thin, unfed. She is sitting bolt upright in a chair and hopes that he will sit. He has a scarf around his neck for his sore throat, one of hers which he found under the stairs, cream with black fringe. The drink tastes warm and sweet; it is like melted jelly going down her throat, then coursing back into her head, inducing a kind of bravura.

"I lit the fire and the lamp, because it's my house again. You've gone," she says.

"I should have gone," he says solemnly, and mentions the cough that detained him.

"Imagine, it was here all these years," she says, holding up the bottle of port, grey-black with mildew and sheathed in thick, glutinous cobweb.

"Where was it?"

"God knows . . . I used to hide drink from my husband," she says, almost regretfully.

"Was James a drinking man?" he asks; then giving some inaudible toast, he has his first sip.

"The wrong kind of drinking man," she says, and in the shaking of her head is the reinvoking of all their pointless years of spleen.

"I've seen that . . . I've been in houses where the woman is glad to have you there. It keeps the man from harming her."

"Do you go back to these houses?"

"To some."

"To these women?"

For a moment he looks affronted and then shakes his head and says, "Nothing, nothing like that . . ."

"Ever?"

"You see, I still live with my wife. She's . . ." But he cannot bring himself to say that she is in the room. Instead, he stares into the distance, at the lamp, the red walls, so picturesque, and the old soda siphons in their metal basketing, like heirlooms, silvering the space around them.

"How did you know my husband's name?" she asks, and for a second he is embarrassed, the thin neat lines on his forehead meshing, as if being scored with a knife.

"A young lad . . . came from around here . . . Padraig. He told me how your husband got killed."

"Padraig?"

"Paud . . . He came North . . . Reddish hair . . . Excitable. He was in a house I was in once. He described this house very well . . . even this room. Said you adopted him . . . Were his second mother. He called you Cliadhna, Queen of the Munster Fairies. He worshipped you."

"He always got things wrong."

"Still, his heart is in the right place."

"And your heart?" she asks abruptly.

"Home . . . To be up home . . . To be back there."

"Can you not go home?"

"No," he says, his voice inflectionless.

"What's there?"

"The graves are all there. The father, the wife, the child, the brother . . . Everything's there."

"So you're all alone?"

"I'm used to it." All of a sudden he starts to whistle. She sees it as some kind of token, a long, sustained whistle, an air she dimly knows, rich and rousing and mournful.

"What is it called?" she asks, and bows slightly to show her gratitude.

"The Holy Ground—

You will sail the salt seas over
And then return for sure
To see again the ones you love
And the Holy Ground once more.

"You could give it all up . . . and lead a life."

"I know that," he says, and pauses as if to think on the two different existences, the fields and the sheds and the guns; or the inside, a safe inside.

"Eat something," she says, pushing the plate of sandwiches forward.

"Thanks a million" is what he says, but he does not touch them.

"You eat like a bird," she says.

"Hunger is one of the last things you feel."

"And what is one of the first?" she asks, and waits.

"You're getting the better of me," he says, but does not tell her what. He looks at her then, without taking his eyes off her, and adds, "Don't think I wouldn't like things like this. Warmth and food and company. I like it here now . . . Many's the night I've gone past a house and looked in and wished."

"Do you feel hate?" she asks.

"I can't say it's hate," he says. "But the British Army is in our streets and it's wrong. Say what you will, it's wrong . . . What do you think would happen if Irish soldiers patrolled their streets and their shires?"

"What's that?" she says, he says, their words overlapping. With a lightning rapidity he is up, grabbing hold of her and drawing her face downward to the floor, telling her to put her hands over her head. They hear it again, the creak of a window catch being opened.

"Do they shoot or do they call out?" she whispers.

"You're all right," he says, his bare arms strong and supple over hers and his breathing light and winnowy.

From the plastered cornice come two wasps, zzzeeing and chasing each other in crazed, half-asleep frenzy.

"Oh, what fools," she says, but remains for a moment in his grasp, within something, within reach of the murmur of him.

"Oh God, Matt," Cormac says, abashed.

"What?"

"He's touching her."

"What? Where?"

Together now they jockey for it, each pushing the other aside to get a glimpse, each able to reassure the other that yes, they're on the ground, the woman and the boyo. A man about to do a grim and grisly deed having a bit of last-minute fun with the woman.

"Oh, the Biddy . . . Oh, the Biddy," Matt says as he sees them fall to the floor and the man's arms come around her.

"I want to see," Cormac says, huffed at being pushed aside.

"Are you married?"

"I have a girlfriend."

"You understand the nature of the question . . . Are you married?"

"Kind of," Cormac says, and quotes the song about *Birds do it*.

"It's repulsive," Matt says, and hits the telescope in rage.

"He's some Valentino," Cormac says, nuzzling in to have another look.

"It's an orgy . . . an orgy," Matt says, and together they watch the two bodies rise, then caper around the room, meeting and parrying like lovers.

"Get ready," he says, ridding himself of the confines of the heavy jacket and stretching to take the sleep out of one of his legs.

"What do we do, Matt?"

"You fire your cylinders . . . That's what you do, that's what you're paid for," he says, taking the gun from his holster and with his spare arm flinging off the roof of briar and branches that was their blind.

"We better let them out," McGreevy says, and twisting a bit of newspaper he chases them as they float down, then up again, streaking the air, disappearing into the plastered scrolls and garlands of the cornice, whipping and whirling in violent outrage, at flush with the open window, but retreating from the cold, then lost to him, so that he lunges, making diverse and useless leaps, all the while cursing them and cursing his own incompetence.

"A hive of bees stung me once," he says.

"Where was that?"

"West-Meath." Said like that, it could be any man out at night, going to a dance or a card game.

The cold air comes in like a presence, clear, liquid, bracing. The very idea that they were so alarmed, so unnerved, has made them garrulous, that and the air, so beautiful, so piercing. Out there she is able to say what could not be said inside.

"When you lost your wife, was that when you panicked?"

"No . . . It was when I was brought handcuffed to see my Kitty . . . They searched the coffin and the habit for explosives and then they let me look in to say goodbye to her, but I couldn't. I thought, Feck this, if they think this is compassion, they have another guess coming."

"Are your wife and child the nearest to you?"

"Ah no . . . You see, the mother . . ." and in the delicacy of the admission she glimpses the hidden source of him.

"How many years have you been in jail?"

"Fifteen going on sixteen . . . So far."

"The Ireland you're chasing is a dream . . . doesn't exist anymore . . . It's gone. *It's with O'Leary in the grave.*"

"No one in their right mind wants my life and I am in my right mind," he says. Something stubborn and young and alone and tender about him then as he looks at her with a smile, as if there is something he especially wishes to say. What is that something.

The oil in the lamp is almost used up, a bit of crimson jellied scum clinging to the glass base, and she thinks that presently the light will peter out. She will ask it now.

"Don't go until morning."

"Why do you ask me that?"

"I am asking you."

"Don't ask me"—his tone now abrupt, the eyes flinched and lonely as he thinks that outside, a few fields away, the job and his escape hang in a grave and dicey suspension.

"I'm afraid, Ger."

"Don't ask me things."

"A person could never get close to you . . . no matter how hard they tried."

"Maybe not. We have no one for us, only ourselves." The voice low and lonely and liturgical. The shiver that escapes her then reaches him and comes back to her like some sort of current.

"You're cold," he says.

"It's not the cold," she says, turning away.

She has heard the chains on the stairs, heard them without having to listen for them, the clink-clank starting up in the frigid air beyond the room.

Death has already entered; it is like a black star, a soft black star being hauled up the stairs on its iron shanks.

In the bedroom she cuts her hair. The scissors are quite blunt and she cuts hurriedly and randomly. Grey-black switches fall onto the bed. They look as if they belong to another, a forebear, those gnarled and mawkish people she had always tried to run away from.

She chops and chops, using the fingers of her other hand to locate a lump of it, snare it, snip it, and then consign it to the bed.

Were she to ask herself why she is doing this she would know. At first she does not ask herself, then does. Something he said. How when the fight was over and the country one, he would like children, wains. It did not seem untruthful when he said it, but it did not seem as if it would ever be. And as she heard him say it, a great lunatic fork of longing rose up in her, to be young again, to have wains.

"That's why I'm cutting my hair," she says to the dying light inside her and the shadows within the room, to a world rushing away, with no time for the old and not that much for the young either. Defiance. Chastisement. Or was it a farewell?

Without deliberating she picks a strand, takes it to the tin box in which is hidden the envelope with TO BE OPENED AFTER MY DEATH. She does not have to read what is in the envelope, she knows. Someone will read it one day. Someone will sit on the windowsill and read:

I was not ready for a child. The crib that he brought up from the cellar was the most forlorn-looking thing. It had belonged to his people. It felt alien. I couldn't see myself rocking it. The woman I went to lived twenty miles away. She didn't ask my name. She didn't ask me outright what I wanted, she already knew. Onnie they called her. She had no second name. Her chimney smoked. I was told that was how I would recognise the house, a gate lodge, smothered with yew trees and a chimney that smoked. Bicycled there but not back. Inside, the house and its contents smelt of that smoke. She gave me a dose, brown jollop which I drank from an enamel mug. Then I lay on a cot bed and she got the wire and started to root and unsettle. She said if I roared she'd stop. She gave me a thing to hold. It was a mesh basket with a false eggshell inside it and when pressed the shell parted and a chicken popped up and squeaked, a yellow cloth chicken. I tried to imagine that the wire was skewer-

ing its gullet instead of me. My whole insides were raw. If I screamed or roared she would stop. She told me so. I pressed the mesh dozens of times and the chicken piped up. Then I heard something gush inside me, like a dug well. I did not think of my husband. He was away. Little do we know. Little do we know. She had a man to drive me back, the bicycle tied to the roof.

The Brid one smelt a rat. She saw me come in wobbly and said nothing. She was polishing fire irons. She knocked on the door of the WC and said there was someone outside to see me.

The first blob of blood was thick and dark, like a black beetle that would not go down. It got puce in colour with each flushing. Then the cistern went dry.

"It would never have been right"—that's what I said.

The person outside requesting to see me was a gypsy woman that had been before. I'd given her sandals and cast-offs. The Brid one said that I was to go out and cross her hand with money. She said the thing that was happening would come all right if I crossed that palm with money.

"Give her a shilling," I said.

"I haven't got a shilling," Brid said.

"Give her whatever we have."

Afterwards she had to draw buckets of water from the pump and leave them outside the door. She knew.

"Can you come out, missus," she begged.

I bled like a pig. She brought towels, first one, then another. She helped me upstairs. We make our beds and we lie on them, our swamped beds.

Mile after mile of it, dualways, tarred roads, dirt roads, then the mountain road not wide enough for two carts to pass. Ross hated the countryside. The minute he left the city or the suburbs he felt rotten, missed shops and prams and the smell of fish and chips. Not a clue where he was going. Called up at very short notice; always like that for a tough one. Wild country and getting wilder by the minute. Why would anyone live here or having left it ever want to return? Cottages swamped in dark and dogs like mad hyenas running after the jeep, barking and then giving up. Big dump of rubbish. Mountains brushing the sky. No light, only dark and gloom. A graveyard with tall tombs, tumbling into a town. They face each other, eight men in all, four on each narrow bench. Guard Foley, who knows the countryside, points out landmarks: waterfalls, an asylum, pubs named after famous men, hurly players or patriots.

"You see that pub," he says, and points to a gloomy, yellow, rained-on building at a godforsaken crossroads. They look.

"There's two bullet holes in there, where the 'Tans shot through a toilet door . . . Shot a man dead." Bits of history, bits of folklore; each man taut with suspense but not showing it openly, showing it in different ways, a tic, a shrill laugh, the maddening mashing of a Coca-Cola tin; the man only just married wishing to be inside in bed with the wife, others who wouldn't miss it for anything, their adrenaline up. The low hills and fields like patchwork of ground, parcelled between the stone walls. Godforsaken.

Ross is next to a young Guard, same age as himself, but they haven't spoken; the man opposite him seems to be pondering something crucial. Others are deferential to this man, keep repeating his name—Sergeant Cleary—deferring to him, though he is silent. He cannot speak. He is thinking of the last time and now this time. Two missions in a matter of months.

"I'm the only man here to have shot one of them," Cleary says to himself, and knows that Foley knows and looks up to him for it. But Foley does not know everything. He does not know for instance that his little girl, Dolores, asked him if it was real bullets he used and cried when he said yes. No one knows what he felt when he was doing it and what he felt just after when he saw the guy on the road, his getaway car gone, dead and not dead, brain dead but moving and breathing. Tried to put it out of his mind, to black it out, and did except that on occasion, that wedding, when he had had a drink too many and someone sang "Kevin Barry":

Kevin Barry was a young man,
A young man was he.
Kevin Barry gave his young life
For the cause of liberty.

The songs get to one. He'd do it again. He might have to do it before daybreak. The chief superintendent had picked him for the vanguard because of being such a good shot. A lone gunman and a woman. Four Englishmen, forestalled, and twenty or thirty Irishmen heading for the battle zone. A lone gunman and a woman. He might use her, bring her out onto a landing or haul her up on a roof. She had grown fond of him. Happens again and again. Women—softies. The superintendent had filled him in, had phoned him just before midnight to say breakfast is on. Breakfast. That was the code. He felt queasy.

"You see that lake . . . I caught a mussel there . . . But it was a swan mussel. I couldn't eat it," Guard Foley says.

"I'd like a bit of help with the clues," another Guard, Fogarty, says.

"There seems to be a lot of lakes up here," a strange Guard says.

"Piles of them . . . We're renowned for them," Guard Foley says, and points to the water and the water birds and the tender reeds and the beauty of it all.

"*Sea God. Small piece of toast or biscuit with savoury top-*

ping. Ko the Ma who ran wild in a frenzy," Guard Fogarty says, giving the first three clues.

"Neptune," Guard Hanrahan shouts, and the name of the sea god is written into place.

"What's your name?" Ross asks his friend quietly.

"Conor . . ."

"Where were you born?" Ross asks.

"Ballyglass, West Cork."

"Is that the Gaeltach?"

"No, but it's not far."

"My aunt went to the Gaeltach once and brought back periwinkles . . . We had a cousin, a nun, there."

"Canapes," someone else shouts and the second clue is written into place.

"What the hell are canapes? Are they a fruit?"

"You've never heard of canapes . . . You're a bog man."

"They're things with things on them . . . My favourite is a prawn. A Dublin Bay prawn," the crossword man says, and dampens his puce pencil while he luxuriates in the unblemished girlish colour and the flirty look of the little pink thing, curling, looking neither dead nor alive.

"There are no Dublin Bay prawns anymore," he is told.

"How do you know?"

"The water's all sewerage . . . It stinks."

"Devilled prawns," Guard Fogarty says, and ponders the third clue, which is a bugger.

"Feck."

"Fecking Jaysus."

"Oh Mother of God."

Expletives as they are thrown to the floor, the jeep clogged in a ditch and the driver's forehead glued to the windscreen. They each think the same thing. The Supremo has struck ahead of them. Conor is the first to see that it is a deer sprawled over the bonnet, a roe, bounding from one hedge across to the next, possibly as it had done every morning, believing the lonely countryside to be its milieu.

"Are you all right, Mossie?" he says, as he pulls the driver upright and pats his face, Mossie all the while mouthing apologies, how it was so sudden, invisible, like an apparition.

"You're all right," Conor says again and again, and offers him a hand outside.

The expletives are the same as they all pile out but uttered now in amazed and high-pitched relief.

"It beats all . . . It beats all." They stare at her, a young doe, stunned but kicking, red sockets flooded with a kind of idiotic trustingness.

"She's badly hurt," Conor says.

"Lift her down," Sergeant Cleary says.

"If you don't mind, Sergeant . . ." Conor pauses to make sure that he is not being insolent, then states his preference, which is to incapacitate her immediately.

"Why?" the sergeant asks.

"She's bleeding internally . . . She's dying inside," he says, and gets the okay from the sergeant to do it.

Without having to deliberate, he knows which gun to select, and with the stock under his arm, he aims at the heart placidly, tenderly, like a young man in a rustic painting. Two shells, each sounding to Ross like a pig's bladder being burst, and the creature itself stock-still, having no time to struggle or buck.

"We'll clean her up now," he says, as if it's his duty to console them. The knife, grazing the suede of her stomach between her front legs, cuts deftly, and the quick delicate spatters of blood that come out seem not like the consequence of death at all but life-giving totems seeping back into the road that was ruddy from mountainy rain.

After he has been sick, Ross buries his face in the hedge, drinks it in, loves the pure feeling of it, like sinking in a casket of liquid diamonds.

"Does it always sound like that, Conor?" he asks as the young man comes up to see to him.

"Like what?"

"That throb."

"What throb?"

"When the bullet enters the flesh."

"I don't know . . . Probably."

"It sounded so odd . . . so cushiony."

"That's because shellfire is loud and hard."

"You know a lot about firearms."

"We had guns as a child at home. We used to shoot snipe. She felt nothing, that roe."

"How do you know?"

"Lead travels faster than the speed of light . . . The bullet is in before they know it."

"Is it the same with a human?"

"Please God," and the two of them bending down to wash their hands and faces in the stream are like penitents giving thanks for something difficult and seeking intercession for something fateful that is to be.

They stand in a packed room now while the detective superintendent gives them the final briefing. He walks as he does it, tall, grey-haired, a restless man who when he meets a table or a chair puts his legs over it and leaps it like a lurcher. Maps everywhere, maps and aerial photographs which he points to. He remarks on the windows of the house, the exits, the terrain all around, the trees, the old woodland and then symmetric lines of young forest where the subversive would go, except that he adds he would have to be a pretty smart cookie to get away. He remarks on the morning being frosty, the ground therefore harder, the likelihood of skidding; to talk as little as possible and to exercise great care, to be on the watch for booby traps or explosives of any kind.

They are already delegated, three to four men for every officer in charge, men at the front gate, men up along the road, men at the lower gate, flanks of men ringed around the house itself, and the vanguard, whose job it is to rush in and take him by surprise. Nothing else to be said except to go for it, to work as a team, to liaise with others at all times, to exercise caution and not rule out the fact that there might be a second gunman not known to intelligence.

"Well, lads," he says then, and glances so he is on eye level with each one, but rapidly so that their eyes do not meet.

"Let him know you mean business," and with that he grasps the arms of the two men, Cleary and Browne, on whom the success of the operation rests.

"Mind yourselves," he says as they file out. A loneliness in it, the ache of a man hoping that all the planning and all the strategy will not be in vain.

"Sh . . . Sh . . . Shiona." She is standing behind his chair, his dead wife, his murdered wife, about to place her hand on his nape. He waits for her to do it; his skin is hot and shivery, waiting for her touch. He waits. The moment so beautiful and so full of suspense. He does not turn round. He cannot bear to see her face, her beautiful long sad face that always made him cry. As soon as he touches her neck he will turn and pull her face down towards him and bury himself in the crevice of her breasts. He thinks he is not dreaming; he thinks he is up, putting his trousers on and pushing down the button of the alarm clock that the woman loaned him. He is in a different bed. The woman insisted that he come upstairs to a warmer room, and he remembers the sheetless bed and the woman throwing something over the mattress and then bringing in an eiderdown and standing over him with the lamp and the clock, like a nurse, a nursing mother. A good woman to him.

Time to go. All that stops him is Shiona. Waiting for her to touch him, to be his protection. He thinks he is up, but he is dreaming.

"The final furlong," Sergeant Slattery says, flanked by his team of four. Ross is among them.

Their pace so quiet, so solemn and furtive. They cling to the hedges, the hedges hooped with briars, sheathed and limned in mist. There is so little light that the crows rising, scudding, and then trotting along the grass are like sturdy young turkeys. Over to one side an unbroken belt of winter trees, all meshed together in a sort of plum-coloured haze, then the evergreens, mile after mile of young forestry which if he reaches it, is sweet and fulsome cover.

Ross thinks the drops of dew along the telephone wires are like rosary beads that a nun sent him. He is separated from Conor and wishes he wasn't. They could give each other gumption. His rifle feels light, everything is light, his head too, as if puffballs are being powdered into it. He prays that he will not disgrace himself when the crunch comes.

Coming on the house so blue and beautiful but lonely from disuse, he gasps. A hush to it—the blotched and weathered walls, the birds' nests dangling from the eaves, and the creeper so assiduous that the tiny dark threads clinging to the mortar resemble scrollwork, tracing its battered history, which the morning will substantiate.

" 'Tis a pity to hurt her," he says, staring at it.

" 'Tis what these psychopaths want, to kill everything of beauty we have," Foley says.

"Sssh. Stealth, lads, stealth," the sergeant says.

A blackbird with yellowish beak ajar sits watch on a low limb of a tree, and inside, the two dreamers dream on rampantly.

Dreams are gone now, aborted in this summons to fire. A posse of men like a hunting party, except there are no beaters and no dogs. In every jawline a setness, a gravity betokening this appointment with mortality. How incongruous it all seems, the loaded machine guns, the loaded rifles, the brilliant glitter of frost, soft mildewed sugarplums on the fruit trees, and men like phantoms moving to their positions. How long will it take? Two, three minutes of hectic discharge, or maybe he will give himself up?

The hinges of the front door yield to the sledge, and like a drunken effigy the door itself swings back quietly, admitting Sergeants Cleary and Browne and the two men who are covering for them.

"Come down, McGreevy . . . Come down . . . We know you're there." He wakens to it, this pleasant country voice through a hailer, and he remembers the night before: the woman, their conversation, the hot toddies, and he jumps from his strange bed and he thinks, I had a chance . . . I had a fecking chance and I blew it.

The first three shots from his revolver punch through the painted panelling of her husband's bedroom and volley to the landing outside.

"If you shoot again we will have to return fire."

With that quick articulation of mind and body and with the wizardry that is native to him, he depresses the trigger of his rifle, firing a full magazine in one continuous blast, aiming in different and disparate directions to confuse them, and thinks that maybe there is one last chance to crawl to a valley gutter in the roof hidden under a mound of slate.

"Flush him out."

"Flush him out."

"Man the skylight."

Men in the hall, men scaling the stairs, the voices at once bold and cursory and savage. Everywhere the sharp tone of fire, tat-tat-tat, tat-tat-arra, in ones, twos, threes, the pattern so regular and swift, and blithe, then the clumsy slump of falling plaster and bats roused from their sleep, moving in a frenzied choreography.

When she wakens, she already knows what she must do. Drawing on an old raincoat she hurries out, barefoot. They must not kill him. She must remonstrate with them, mediate between him and them, which is perhaps why he came to her rather than another. She will see to his deliverance. On the top landing, the pall of gunsmoke and the rapid gleeful charge of gunfire down below do not frighten her at all; she feels impervious to it, determined to find him, but finds instead in her husband's bedroom the gutted panelling and the gruesome gluey front where a wardrobe mirror had been.

The sounds of the artillery are in some way less frenzied than the sounds of the men. A phalanx of them run to the rear of the house in answer to some urgent summons there. They move not like mortals at all but like gods, letting out fierce and godly warlike sounds. By contrast the tut-tut of fire is calm, mathematical, almost measured. She calls, but no one hears her or looks in her direction. It is as she stands on the next landing and hesitates that Guard Foley glimpses her through a long stained-glass window, a figure moving in the gloamy light of pre-dawn, a silhouette in a raincoat with closely cropped hair.

"There's a second gunman . . . a second gunman," he says, and asks a comrade to come and look, but she has moved away.

"You're sure?"

"I saw him . . ."

The woman has no fear. She is calling as she moves, groping through this wilderness of smoke. He must be taken alive. His life has many chapters to it and many evolutions. They do not know that. But she knows it, because she knows him. On the forelanding as she enters the second bedroom a congregation of reeling bats gives her more cause for alarm than the ceaseless crackle which she still feels separate from. Hearing them up on the roof and believing that they have cornered him, their voices so queerly inhuman and hysterical, she crosses to shout out. Halfway she is stopped in weird and pantomimed suspension as the floor gives way and she falls, thinking and knowing that she has fallen and is merely injured. A shower of bullets like a swarm of crazed insects whiz back and forth around her, then one colliding with a second one, mid-course, rebounds and wings towards her, while her mouth, opening to say, but then non-say, is struck speechless as the metal leech is sucked violently and unerringly into the maelstrom of her unfinished plea. Her legs and her lower half drop through the ceiling, where she dangles like some grotesque trapeze artist, while Sergeant Slattery down below, without even having to touch her, knows that it is a woman, that it is the shins and toes and bunion of a woman, utters a "Sweet Jesus," and then, with the abandon of a madman, shouts at them to stop, to stop firing because the woman has been injured.

Voices, scuttling, pandemonium all drowned in the almighty crash as a balustrade comes tumbling down. Biding his moment, McGreevy waits inside a swathe of evergreen, creeping from branch to branch like Mad Sweeney in the poem.

"Shut your . . ." he says to the crows in idiot consternation around him, while ahead his deliverance, acres of pine and spruce, an eel of dark through which he will slither and vanish. Then, with a disbelieving intake of breath, he senses another, as through the lacework of frosty green he sees the rifle breaching the cover and a boggled face within a foot of him.

"Where do you think you're going, McGreevy?" The tremour in the voice an indication of astonishment. One last chance.

In a panting silence they wrestle, each with his spare hand, struggling with and staving off the other, like animals locked in a sort of primeval maul, until he gains supremacy, knees the scut into the basin of the tree, and prepares to strip him of his rod, when Nature, the bitch, betrays him and he slips from the wet mossy bough onto the ground, with the suppleness of a sack.

"Oh Jesus Christ, nail him," the voice says, and then a bullet grazes his ankle, then rushes past him into a tree stump, which leaps into the air before bursting into shreds.

"He's going nowhere . . . His karma is up." It is Rory's beaming face congratulating the young Guard that had sniffed him into the tree.

They rush at him then, shouting orders to drop his weapon, to put his hands up, to lie face down, frisking his thin body through his vest and jeans and scrutinising the face for fear or shame or shock, or anything. The flesh of his face stretched against his temples is that of someone just converted into wire.

"He's down, lads . . . He's down, lads." The words said with such gusto, passing from one to another, reaching the group inside the house, then a boastful answering echo as blatant as cock crow. The click of the handcuffs is like that of a key turning inside his skull, turning in on all of him, the old journeys and the one ahead, the cubic dungeon.

Eight or nine faces, gaping, gawking, a jubilation that is not like the several sounds of men but single-throated, the voice of vindication, the taunt of the land, the land that he was pledged to since birth.

He seems to be watching, but without communion with them, or with the earth, and none with the stretcher onto which he is being lifted, the burning in his ankle a relief in some way and the blobs of half-melted frost, dripping from the trees, like tears or holy water being sprinkled on him.

"Get the fucker out . . ." It is Rory's voice, full of hate and urgency, repeating it at an ever-increasing pitch. Inside, the ambulance was dark and snug; he felt safe, safe from their racket and safe from their insults, tucked in like a tray of bread, his leg agony but safe, and then the raw daylight again, being laid on the grass and feet stalking over him.

He can feel the dew, he can skim it with his fingers. What he sees is the woman being brought on a litter, a bead of blood like a wood strawberry on her temple, fresh, bright, edible, and a young Guard keening over her.

Cormac, the Guard, leans in, saying the same thing, the same sorry thing, while his friend Ross pulls him back, insisting that it was not his fault, not his fault at all, that it could happen to anyone, a blasted bullet that ricocheted up through the ceiling and went haywire.

"That's the down end of it," Sergeant Slattery says.

"That and a cock-up of intelligence," another says.

"How can there be so little blood?" Cormac asks, and then howls it to the unslept ring of faces, who though they pity him are as well basking and rejoicing in that terrific pent-up exultance of men who have done something dangerous together. He asks it of the crows with their watery, pitiless eyes, and the centuries-old walls green and grieving from the elements; asks why a bullet that struck and killed would then decide to stay in there, to live in there, like some freak.

"I knew her well," Guard Gallagher says, and kneels by her as a relative might to catch her dying declaration. But there is none. No one will ever know her last thought or her last word; all they see is a woman with a face pale as the albumen inside an eggshell, the berry of blood, a stilled twitch around the mouth, suggesting an unfinished utterance.

"No fool like an old fool," Matt says, and thinks how he saw something no one else saw: lewd, disgusting, the pair of them on the floor writhing, then going out to finish it off. What was she now telling her Maker?

"She had to die," a sergeant says, a tall man who is holding a sprig of shiny laurel in his hand. For what? For Ireland. For martyrdom. For feck-all. Voices asking but no voice answering, only the crows, unnerved by the racket, wheeling and whirling in crazed circuits.

"She gave him sanctuary . . ." the sergeant says, and solemnly slips a bit of greenery between the crook of her folded hands as if into a statue. At that moment a bird, not a crow, dips down and seems to sip from the blood before flying off again.

"That's no ordinary bird," a young nurse says, and asks them to kneel to say an Act of Contrition. Cormac cannot kneel and cannot pray. He would go into the forest and shoot himself, except that they have taken his gun for debriefing.

"There was men shooting everywhere and I shot too . . . I thought it was my job." He yells it so that it carries across the fields peopled with thistles and up the road to the village where the news is just filtering.

"Stop crucifying yourself," Sergeant Slattery says, and others assure him that it is not his fault but the fault of the man, the scum, lying there with not a single tear in his eyes. They converge on him now. Some stoop as if they could see into him, see into the sick mind and transcribe it for others. His face is blank and powdery, as if dusted with talcum, and the veins on his handcuffed wrists are blue and furious and curdled.

"A sicko that held the country hostage," one says, and Rory nods, remembering his little girl, Aoife, having the fits, talking in her sleep, his wife sleepwalking, the whole family sparring.

"Not much over five foot seven," Guard Foley says, and walks the perimeter of the stretcher to make sure he is not far off.

"Wonder he didn't bite you," Matt says, recalling a fellow captured near Nenagh who bit into the thigh of a Guard, bit through his clothing. Different voices, different gestures, some who would like to kick him to death then and there, others would like to see him hang; one, the tall sergeant with the sprig of green, would like to ask him just one question: What made him what he is?

"I knew a schoolteacher of yours," he says despairingly. No answer.

"A tadpole," Matt says, and kicks one of the bare feet. It was as if he had not heard and never would. He lay there alone and motionless, enclosed in a thin nimbus of rain, his eyes looking upwards and backwards at a few wan stars dissolving back into the heavens.

"Ah, our knight in shining armour," Sergeant Slattery says when he sees the detective superintendent emerge from his car and cross quickly to look first at the woman inside the ambulance and say something to the nurse. He nods then to each of his men, singling out no one in particular, while knowing of course that it was Cormac who fired the fatal shot and would know it anyhow by the hung head and the pink hands pawing the atmosphere for mercy.

"We've had great success and great sadness," he says, and then crouches to say something to McGreevy. The men nudge and stiffen—two supremos who had tracked each other like polar animals, through bogland and mountain and quarries, face to face at last. He can hardly believe it, that this slight man who seemed to all the embodiment of twenty men is lying there in jeans and an orange vest with a sun god on it. He remembers the night he chased him in Wexford and lost him on Vinegar Hill, and lost him the next morning in a gypsy encampment, where a woman stopped him, strewed branches to trip him up. He remembers everything, the hours and hours of overtime, the phone calls, no sleep, not even being able to go to his sloop to think, clues, half clues, all consummating in this spectral tableau.

"Are you cold?" he asks. There is no answer. There is only the still shape, as though he had been cast there.

His men watch the superintendent walk away, thin and haggard, his hands behind his back, a terrible gravity to him as he approaches the house. Through the missing doorway he sees the battered and pitted walls, the stairs askew, with a hat-stand wrapped around it and an old fur coat hanging jauntily off. Inside is worse. In the back where the explosive went off, wood, metal, and glass are in weird configurations, remainders of wall wobbling like loose teeth in a gum and a fierce and innocent mass of paint where a picture of Christ and the Virgin has been splashed and muralled into a wall.

"It could have been a bloodbath," one of the forensic men says. With the tapes and cameras they are retracing the lines of fire, tracking where the bullets came from, where they went, mapping the progress of the woman going from room to room, and he thinks that the grimmest job of all is measuring death's furrow. He will have to answer for her death to the powers that be and answer to himself. The young lad will have to answer too. A young lad who should not have been in that spot at that moment and a man lying on a stretcher with the cold unswerving conviction of a Messiah. Human error. Human cruelty. Hungry cawing crows.

"It could," he says to the man, looking up through the holes in the ceiling at bits of sky, at the brazen sun and the brazen day, hearing the ambulance siren starting up, then mounting, that despairing yodel that he always thought of as being half bird, half animal.

His anger is up now, the beauty and lineaments of the house utterly destroyed, a woman dead, and another notch in the so-called struggle. He stands above McGreevy, possessed of a cold and furious determination to smash through that lashing radius of hate and fanaticism to get to him. He knows that within the wrenched and torn sockets of his reasoning there is some kind of conscience and accountability that sets him apart, a seriousness that makes others look up to him, that singles him out, and that gives him the blind impervious aura of the martyr.

"You could have done a lot for your cause and your country, McGreevy . . . but all you done was death upon death upon death." The figure does not stir or respond, seems to be slipping away into invisibility, like a shoreline at evening receding into the identically coloured pale sky.

"Are we to take him to the station?" Guard Gallagher asks.

"No. They're waiting for him in Dublin," the detective sergeant says, and waits even then for some quiver, some prehension, some reflex, but there is none. He lay there alone and motionless, like a child who has just been dispatched to an alien world.

"So it's back to the old academy," one of the Guards says

as two of them lift him under the armpits and towards the maw of the Black Maria. They had met years earlier when he had handcuffed him at the border and had inquired about the colour of his eyes, since there was some dispute about them, and had been told wryly that they were green, but did it matter? It was different now, cold and spiteful. Trust had gone out of the land and out of the people; the old wars, the old atrocities had been replaced with crookeder and bitterer ones, and brother no longer gasped at the bloodshed of brother.

"I'd say thirty years," the second Guard says in a bluff voice, and bends over him to study those ungazing eyes and that stupid little scarab of a tattoo.

In thirty years what will he be. Who will he be. Will the land be sated. Will his heart be heavy. Or will everything continue just as it is.

The Child

It's months now. The spring came a week early, the air lost its bite, it was like honey. Petals, white petals and yellow petals, spattered with pollen, blew all over the ground. Even the stones of the fields and the boulders looked less angry. Soft. A plumpness to them. The trees very friendly and green, especially the horse chestnuts with long tassels on them like candles. I'd love to see them lit.

People opened their windows. In the big house it wasn't necessary. The walls and windows gone and the inside and outside all one. The birds have made nests in there and animals trounce around, bits of furniture and pictures and stair rods flung out on the grass. It's awaiting jurisdiction, probate it's called. I peeped in. I didn't go in. People came to gawk more than to mourn. The nurse took my mother's belongings in a suitcase but wore the coatee with the velvet collar, sported it. I thought my mother's death would grant me my life, but it hasn't. The way the soldier thought that to take an Englishman's life would compensate for centuries of wrong; but how could it? The soldier's heart was full of dark and violent thoughts, but the English had no hearts when it came to us. When my mother lay dying she cried out. When we take life we cry out in one voice, but when we lose it we cry out in another. Two chords that must meet. How often seeing her in one of the rooms, in front of a mirror or buffing her nails, I begrudged her her life and her beauty, I wished her dead. She's dead now and buried with it, and the soldier will be an old man before he walks the fields again.

The mountains change colour at night and get solemn, the way the people change when the shooting starts. Everything is drastic then. Everything is riddled. The doer and the done-to. "As the killer is close to him whom he kills." From the near and the far past a wailing and a gnashing. Graves and mounds and more graves and a statue and a dyed carnation to mark where the sudden carnage has been. It weeps, the land does, and small wonder. But the land cannot be taken. History has proved that. The land will never be taken. It is there. "As the killer is close to him whom he kills." That's in a book. But to be close in body or bayonet is not enough. To go in, within, is the bloodiest journey of all. Inside, you get to know—that the same blood and the same tears drop from the enemy as from the self, though not always in the same proportion. To go right into the heart of the hate and the wrong and to sup from it and to be supped. It does not say that in the books. That is the future knowledge. The knowledge that is to be.